Whatever Happened at Leary High?

Whatever Happened at Leary High?

David V. Mason

Northwest Publishing, Inc.
Salt Lake City, Utah

Whatever Happened at Leary High?

This is a work of fiction.
All characters and events portrayed in this book are fictional,
and any resemblance to real people or incidents is purely coincidental.

For information address: Northwest Publishing, Inc.
6906 South 300 West, Salt Lake City, Utah 84047
JC 7.18.95 / JP

PRINTING HISTORY
First Printing 1995

ISBN: 1-56901-812-X

NPI books are published by Northwest Publishing, Incorporated,
6906 South 300 West, Salt Lake City, Utah 84047.
The name "NPI" and the "NPI" logo are trademarks belonging to
Northwest Publishing, Incorporated.

PRINTED IN THE UNITED STATES OF AMERICA.
10 9 8 7 6 5 4 3 2 1

To OUR FRIEND
A Bishop DiNARDO.
May God Bless
you & your ministry!

This book is dedicated to
my father and mother.

The "ClergyGuys"
REV. DAVID V. Mason
Feb 24, 2005

ph. 713.722.9298
DAVIDVMASON@YAHOO.COM

Part One

One

If you've never seen anybody dead before, let me tell you about it. It's not what you think. Now I'm not talking about a beautiful, laid-out stiff like they got over at Mallory's Funeral Home. I mean a dead seventeen-year-old babe at my school—Sue Anne Chadwick. Last week she was a skinny junior with braces and blond pigtails who was real good at math. Wanted to go to college. She was a little weird like a lot of us here at Leary School, but she didn't stick out or anything.

When I saw her yesterday behind the Bronston Tower at the back of the school, her body was all twisted and tangled up. Her face was smashed and something bloody was sticking out of her cheek. Her head was going one way, her chest was going another way—her arms and legs were all exposed and sprawled out in every direction. The concrete was cracked beneath her where she hit and there was a little puddle of blood around her head.

I don't even want to talk about her eyes. Let's just say it's not like it is in the movies.

Our high school is a little different. How different? I guess it depends on who you talk to. Some just say it's a special school—a place for those of us who didn't make it at the city's high schools for some reason. Like doing drugs, skipping school too much or getting in some kind of trouble. They call it an "alternative school." At least that's what Dr. Nealon, our headmaster, calls it here at Leary. He also says it means that if the students could find any alternative to being here, they'd take it.

Everybody knows about this place. My buddy Tommy Elkins told me that Leary used to be a monastery or something a long time ago and then it became a city high school about twenty years ago. But when a new school, Lamar High, was built they were going to tear down this place. Back then it was called Nathan Hale High School—after that Revolutionary War guy. Then the State Mental Health Board rented the thing out for a couple of years and put some real crazies in here— I'm talking super head cases and freaks.

But the state school was just temporary—in a year and a half the state had built a new hospital and sanitarium up in Hitchings and the old school was empty again—that is, until the Leary School—"an alternative secondary education for youth" (it actually says that on the school seal) started up. That was eight years ago. I've only been here two years but I know that most of the Lamar kids act like they still own this place somehow—like the school and all of us going here now are some kind of retards or head cases they keep around just for laughs.

Sure, things happen around here. More than most places, I guess. But it just seems like people make a bigger deal out of it because it happens here at Leary.

A car gets stolen—it's no big deal. A fight breaks out in the gym—so what? Somebody blows out against a teacher—it happens—the teacher can usually handle it. Probably somebody on medication or all stressed out over his stuff at home. Give him a chance to chill out and everything would be okay.

Me and Tommy had it all figured out. But then came the Sue Anne Chadwick thing—and suddenly I wasn't so sure.

Yesterday I stayed after school and did my English homework. I mean, it was a "mandatory tutorial" (they don't want to call it "detention" anymore) because I was late getting to a few classes. I didn't mind. Shelley Prescott, that good-looking new sophomore, was in there for the same reason. I mean, she was one steady gaze, this babe—light brown hair, blue eyes, a great body—the works. At least I could be around her for a while. After the hour was up I left by the back way. I could just hop the back fence, curl around behind the hedges past the back of Mac's Auto Repair Shop and walk about three blocks to get home. But when I walked back behind the Bronston Tower, there she was—all crumpled up in a heap. She looked like some kind of big rag doll somebody'd thrown there on the old concrete sidewalk.

I ran back into the school and told Mrs. Howard about it. She didn't panic like I thought she would. She told me to go on home out the front way and I did, and as I walked home I watched the ambulance pass me on Windemere heading to the school. It wasn't speeding at all.

This morning, the newspaper headline was:

APPARENT SUICIDE AT LEARY SCHOOL

Sue Anne Chadwick, daughter of Charles G. and Susan Chadwick of Lake Forest Boulevard, was found after her apparent suicide Tuesday afternoon. The body was discovered at the foot of the school's unused tower where it is believed the deceased had jumped that afternoon. Funeral arrangements are pending.

It was really something—so short and cold. That paper was a real rag. Had to be among the worst newspapers of any city in the Southwest. But it's all we've got, so I read it. The only real problem with the article was that they didn't put my name in it. It probably wouldn't impress anybody anyway.

The first thing that happened when I got to school the next day was that I talked to Mrs. Shamlian, the guidance counselor. She was okay.

Was I shocked to see the body?

How did I feel later?

Did I sleep all right that night? Any bad dreams?

Yes, okay, not so great—and I couldn't remember any dreams. I mean, what's the difference?

Then she led me into another room and over to the big table used for faculty meetings. It smelled like teachers in there. There was this big, old guy—a detective on the city police force, she said. Right off the bat I didn't like him. He looked at me like I was a convict or something. He just stared at me for a while and pulled out a sheet of paper from his folder. He cleared his throat and it was like him telling me to shut up because he was going to speak—and I hadn't said a word.

"Trawick Powell?"

"What?"

"That's your name?"

"Yep."

He looked at me funny now, with his head cocked. He had his badge stuck on his wallet in front of him on the desk. Big deal. Did you find the body? Did it move or show any signs of life? Do you always take that way home? Why did you go home that way on Tuesday? Did you know the girl? How well did you know her? What was she wearing? Did you see or hear anyone else in the area at that time? Tell me exactly what you did when you saw the body. What position was the body in? Do you feel that the girl had any reason to jump from the tower? Had she said or done anything unusual in the last two weeks?

I grunted and shrugged—yes, no, I don't know. I just happened to stumble on her. Jeez, I don't live with her. As it went on, I wondered if he really thought that Sue Anne had jumped. All during the questions, he watched my face as he lit up a cigarette—with a NO SMOKING sign right behind him on the wall. I mean, it's not like I'm against smoking or anything, it's just that the smoke was coming right at my face. It made me want to puke when I saw the smoke coming out of that red iceberg of a nose and then I had to smell it.

Then he changed the expression on his face and tried to smile—but it was phony.

"I'll bet you were surprised, huh?"

I looked at the big face, the big yellow teeth beneath the huge overhang with nostrils. I wanted to tell him that it was the fourth dead body I'd seen on that sidewalk in the last week or so. I knew he was testing me—like all adults figure they've got to do. If this was interrogation, I'd make sure my story was short and sweet—less hassle that way. After about twenty minutes, he let me go.

Sure I was surprised to see her like that. Wouldn't you be?

TWO

I was glad to get out of there. It was nine-thirty already and Mrs. Shamlian said I could just go on to my history class with Jenkins. It was really cool—I mean, the way everybody in the halls stared at me, talking under their breath to their friends. Looking at me like I was something special. Yeah, I'm the one who found her—me, Wick Powell. Most of the time people just ignored me, acted like I wasn't really there. Maybe I'm a little short and maybe I don't have the best looking face in the world, but I never pretended to be a hunk model or anything.

When I got into history class, the dozen or so students turned around to look at me. Even King, the coolest dude in

the school turned his head to look me over before he leaned
back in his chair and adjusted his mirrored shades. One of the
junior girls, Terri Druso, hunched up behind him trying to
flirt with him. Tommy and I sat off by the wall. Jenkins was
writing something on the board and right when I sat down
and put my book under my seat, I heard it. It came from
Ferrito, the hot-shot junior dude who was half mental from
drugs.

"Okay, Powell, so tell us—what did she look like?"

I waited a second to think of something. Everybody
turned to me, even Jenkins, nervous about it all.

"It kinda looked like your face, Ferrito."

Everybody laughed. It was funny. Jenkins made us get to
work, but in a few minutes Bobbie Koenig turned and asked
me what it was really like. She opened her eyes wide, expect-
ant and hopeful. She didn't look too bad. Tommy just grinned.
I didn't feel like answering, so I didn't—maybe later. Jenkins
tried to run class as usual, but everybody was stirred up—
they wanted to talk about Sue Anne. They'd done it in their
other classes, so why couldn't they do it in this class? Jenkins
just pushed his glasses up onto his forehead and sort of
massaged his nose.

"If you've been talking about it all morning, why do you
need to talk about it now?"

That made sense. Most of my classes were just organized
boredom, but Jenkins was one of the few teachers at Leary
who actually tried to teach you something. I liked that. I
watched him smooth down the lapels on his old corduroy
jacket as the complaints died down. In my other classes that
afternoon you could just bet that it would be like feeding time
at the zoo. I think most of us have got spring fever pretty bad,
too. By the time the day was over the story would probably be
that twenty kids had jumped from the tower and bounced on
the concrete and got stacked up like a little log cabin.

Jenkins told everybody that if they had any information to add to the investigation they could do it during the lunch break. A few people groaned, but Jenkins just told us that everyone was saddened and mystified by Sue Anne's death, but that we could do nothing now to bring her back.

"What's done is done," he said. "Let's be grateful we are still able to get on with our own lives." So we turned to page 117 and listened to some more about Manifest Destiny.

He tried to make it sound like it should matter to us—that this part of the country was shaped by all that stuff. The pioneers moved the natives out or killed them and they settled here and called it their own. "Run the Indians out or fence them up on some barren land like the Cattawaugas reservation three hundred miles west of here—" he said it ironiclike, "—that's the American way. You want something, you take it, and then you moralize about it later."

He was probably right, but nobody was listening to him. Two girls, Patti Ranc and Felicia Peters, were taking turns using some kind of curling iron in each other's hair and staring into their mirrors. Timmy Malton just laid his head down on his desk.

At lunch, Tommy and I went on out to his car like we usually do. I had packed my lunch and he bought a sandwich and some chips and we sat and ate in the front seat with KQBT playing the hits. His radio was pretty lame but we could still hear it. It was an '82 Dodge—a little rusted out but it looked okay on the outside. We looked around and saw a few other kids sitting in their cars and eating. Three sophomore girls (including Shelley Prescott) were right across from us with Clark Severino, a junior, behind the wheel.

"So, you're a celebrity. How come you're not in there mingling with your adoring fans?"

"Aw, quit it. You know they'll forget all about it by Monday. Anything to get their minds off this place."

He nodded a little as he looked around at the other cars and then opened a window and hung his left arm out. "It's cool…" he said. Whatever "it" is got his approval. It was his famous expression. Maybe not all that original, but when he said it, it sounded right. He had his usual grin on his face, the one that pulled his mouth around funny.

"You hear they've got the suicide prevention squad out here today?"

I looked at him but I couldn't tell if he was kidding or not.

"Really?" I said, "…and they're just in time, too."

We both laughed at that. It seemed pretty grim, though. Sometimes people see somebody kill himself and get all that attention and they hate their own lives so much or they want to get back at their parents so bad that they want to do it too. Only they're so wasted or mental that they don't stop and think that they won't be able to enjoy the attention.

Tommy just shrugged and said the "Suicide Squad" was a bunch of frustrated housewives looking for something to do. None of it mattered. Not a whole lot did matter to Tommy, but I still wanted to know what he thought about it all.

"Do you think she jumped?" He kept eating his chips and thought for a while.

"I doubt it—what'd she have to kill herself over? She was doing all right, wasn't she?"

"I don't know—I thought so. I haven't heard anything about her leaving a note or anything, did you?"

He just shook his head and tapped the side of the car to the beat of the music. "Maybe she stumbled and fell off or something—an accident." Then he shrugged—"Naw, that's stupid. Nobody would go up in the tower and trip looking over the edge."

Tommy was pretty smart, but he didn't realized what he was saying. Between bites of my sandwich, I managed to ask, kind of coollike—"Well, if she didn't jump and she didn't trip—what else is there?"

"I don't know—" Then he turned to me. "Oh, I get it—well, why'd you throw her off the tower, Powell?" He grinned, crumpled up his empty potato chip bag, and then stuffed it into his pocket. He was a very tidy guy.

Over in the car right across from us, big Ruthie Katrana was trying to get over into the back seat but she was being held across the seat and spanked by Shelley and Clark. I guess Shelley was already real popular around the school. Finally, Ruthie slid over onto the back seat and the bad springs made the car bounce around. We could hear the shrieks and laughter from their car. Ruthie was wearing blue jeans, so there was nothing to get excited about.

Then we saw King come walking out to their car, with Smeg and Ferrito walking behind him. Boy, was he easy to spot. Tall, big shoulders—that black leather jacket with kind of punky-looking silver studs on the back. His hair was wild and black, pushed back off his face. His skin was rough, needing a shave, and you never saw his eyes behind the mirrored shades. Never. Smeg had that shaved-head Mohawk and a face that looked like a pepperoni pizza. Ferrito's straggly hair had about every color of the rainbow in it.

Clark practically bolted out of the car to go over and speak to King. King just stood there with his thumbs hitched in his belt loops as he listened to Clark. Then he nodded and walked away. Smeg and Ferrito followed. The others stopped fooling around in the car and watched, but they acted like they weren't.

Tommy said nothing during it all. He didn't have to—we all knew about King. There's a story for you. If the teachers and Nealon ever found out about it—even half of it—they'd probably close the school down and ship him out to the state prison for twenty years.

And I'm not kidding.

Three

The rest of the day went like I predicted—everybody talking about Sue Anne's death, something they knew absolutely nothing about. Three girls got called in to talk to that detective—her best friends in school, I guess. The Citywide Suicide Prevention Services people were going to have an assembly the next day for the whole school. That was predictable too. Like I said, to make sure none of our head cases tried to imitate Sue Anne to get a rush just before they hit the ground.

Somebody noticed that the padlock on the old door that led to the closed-off tower stairs had been jimmied off. A new lock and hinge had been put on. Nobody knew who'd messed with the old one, but it was probably Sue Anne. No one even knew what she was doing staying on the school grounds that day. She didn't have tutorial. Somebody said she was pregnant—that I didn't believe. You heard drugs, booze, pills and throwing herself off the tower because of some guy she was dating. All of it sounded like rumor—people just wanting to say stuff to be on the inside of it all. I actually saw the body first and now I didn't even feel like I was in the know. Some of the guys asked me about it and I told them what I saw. And I told Bobbie Koenig too, because she'd asked me. I told them and that was it. I felt like I had some kind of power—but they wanted to know more and I didn't know anything more, and then I was back to being little Wick Powell, a junior nobody.

My classes were over at three and I walked home out the back way again, around the tower. The whole area had been marked and closed off with yellow tape line that said "PO-LICE LINE—DO NOT CROSS." I looked around, ducked under it and walked home with my history book in my hand. Heading down Kirby Drive under the overpass of Highway 59, I listened to the cars speed over my head before rush hour really got going. I cut across Wood Hollow Drive to our apartment complex—the Pecan Grove apartments. Ours was number twenty-seven.

The walk is only about fifteen minutes and soon I was fumbling around in my pocket for the key. I wasn't in any hurry, because I knew what was in there. Nothing. Mom was out of town on another business trip—she'd been gone five days already. No pets—they weren't allowed in the apartment. Mom had left three big casseroles in the refrigerator before she'd left. I was into the second one already but right now I didn't feel like eating—especially that tuna and noodle casserole. So I just got a cold Coke out and plopped down on the sofa. From there I could see the answering machine. The little red light didn't blink even once, so she hadn't called to leave any more instructions. I knew them by heart. "Come straight home after school—if you go out in the evening, be in by ten-thirty. If you have any questions, call me—" and she always left two or three out-of-town numbers. She'd driven our only car out of town, so even though I'd gotten my license four months ago it didn't do me much good.

In the three years since the divorce, she'd changed. It used to be that she'd give me a full page of instructions that I had to carry around with me at all times. Now, I guess she figured that I was old enough to know what was going on and that I could look out for myself.

She had confidence in me. But there really wasn't much else we could do. Neither one of us liked living in an apartment—maybe we got spoiled by living in our house when Dad was with us. I could take apartment living though—anything was better than having to hear them screaming at each other all the time.

Then I heard it. It was that time again—the weird, unnaturally loud music came right through the walls of the apartment. Even covering my ears didn't help much. It played the same damn tune over and over again—and still again and again. The ice cream truck. Finally, it stopped—and I walked over to the window and watched the kids crowd around to get a treat. The young black man in a white service suit made them all step back and get into a line, and he waited until they stopped pushing and shoving before he would sell them the ice cream treats. The grimy little hands of the kids counted out the coins carefully, some with the help of older brothers and sisters. It was 3:25, right on the dot. It passed this way before going up Kirby Drive and over to the Windemere condos across from the school.

There were times when I stayed after school that I could hear the ice cream truck faintly as it played right here. Far away, it sounded like church bells, soft on the wind. Up close, it sounded like some bizarre air raid siren from another galaxy. But the kids loved it—just loved it. You'd think their entire world revolved around that ice cream truck guy. Who knows? Maybe it does.

I thought about Sue Anne. Did she have any kid brothers or sisters? Were they out there in the excited line of kids waiting for some ice cream? I didn't really lie to the people at the school—I just didn't tell them everything. I'd thought a lot about Sue Anne lying dead in front of me. It kept springing up in my mind. The next time I talked to Mom, I'd tell her about it. It did bother my sleep some and it bothered me when I was awake, too. "You just don't understand death unless you see it." That's what Billy Stephens said once, and I think he's right. (If I didn't already say so, Billy is the psychologist I see once a week.) He knew something about death. And now I've seen death—close up and real—and I still don't think I understand it. It was like it wasn't really Sue Anne there, even though her face and eyes were boring into me. It was like some kind of broken mannequin in a store downtown. The details of it, of the whole scene—were burned into my brain. I don't know how long I stood and looked.

I'm not much for religion or anything, and most of the people I know aren't. For sure, my parents aren't. But I'm telling you, whatever was there in front of me wasn't Sue Anne—it was empty. Whatever was really Sue Anne had left that body. That's why I didn't freak when I saw it. It was sort of peaceful. And whatever happened to that heap of flesh and bones now didn't matter to her or to me, and it probably shouldn't matter to anybody else either. Maybe I'm a little crazy, but that's what I think. I know they're going to dress it up and put it on display for everybody—make her look better in the casket than she ever did alive. If that's what her family wants to do, that's their business. But I really don't think it's right. She's dead—let her be dead. You'd almost have to be some kind of mental to want to pretty up a corpse and talk to it the way people do.

Mrs. Shamlian at the school seemed surprised that I didn't have more of a reaction to it all. I felt it more than I let on—but still not that much. It's just that it keeps popping up in my head. Sue Anne was kind of quiet and proper—had her own little bunch of friends. I'm not even sure why she was at Leary. She was pretty average all the way around, except for being real good at math. The strongest memory I had of her was when she gave an oral report on William Wordsworth in front of the English class. She did a good job and Leslie Wilkerson, the new English student teacher (and my homeroom teacher), said so. But then she asked Sue Anne a simple question about the guy and she couldn't answer it—and it really seemed to upset her. You could see she was starting to cry when she got back to her seat. Like one little question had ruined everything. But that was in the fall.

I never heard anything about her ever trying to hurt herself. The major head cases like that we usually know about, and not from sneaking into the files, either. People just tell you—whether you want to hear it or not. Like Ferrito and Pac Man (I mean, that's all that guy ever wants to do) and T.C., who's already going bald and looks like he's about thirty, and Samantha Bergland, who decided to get out of her mother's car when it was going thirty-five miles an hour. Some brain damage there, for sure. They've all done weird stuff and tried to hurt themselves in the last few years and now they practically brag about it. No kidding—it can get pretty sickening to listen to and see the scars. Me, I'd rather be around people that just aren't too bright—there's more than enough of those at Leary. At least they act normal. In fact, Tommy and I decided one time that we'd even rather be around the space shots—kids like Timmy Malton who just stared off into the air most of the time or talked to themselves. Lately, about half the time,

Timmy's just been putting his head down on the desk. The other half of the time his head might be in the class, or it might be taking a cruise to the far moons of Neptune. When I finished the Coke I let out a humongous belch and felt better.

Suddenly, I wanted to call Shelley Prescott. She was fresh and new to the school. I'd heard people calling her "Missy" recently—I guess because she's so preppy looking. Maybe I could get her to go with me to a movie or something. Yeah. I turned from the window but then I thought of her with those two other sophomore girls giggling together in the car at lunch with Clark Severino. I stopped walking toward the phone when I thought about her being around King and Ferrito a few times. King—how're you supposed to fight that? I mean, the guy looked like he was about twenty-five—a strong, crazy twenty-five at that. Everybody's heard the stories about King getting big money for dealing drugs and all kinds of stuff. He's gotten into bar fights and he ripped a guy's ear off once. I'd heard that King was in a real bad car accident when he was a kid and everybody else died in the car. Now he's not quite right in the head. He never takes off the mirrored shades. I think most of the teachers are scared of him—I mean, they let him get away with murder.

I came back and looked through the window and saw that all the kids had their ice cream and the truck was pulling away as the little ones waved. When it was a good ways down the street that damn music started up again. Still loud and grating. Was that supposed to be a real song, or what?

Well anyway, we had a big, glorious happening—a mystery to liven up the ordinary routine a little. People at Leary aren't stupid. You don't send city police detectives out to interrogate students if it was a suicide. No suicide note, no history of attempted suicide—and we hadn't heard that Sue Anne had anything terrible happen to her recently. The cops think somebody pushed Sue Anne—now they want to know who did it. Maybe the big old guy knew what he was doing. I still think he blew that cigarette smoke in my face on purpose.

By now, they probably know more about Sue Anne than I'll ever know. For sure, they know that she's not a head case or a druggie. And they probably don't classify people the way we do, anyway. As far as I knew, she wasn't a runner, either.

Runner—that's when you run away every once in a while—like me. I'm classified as a runner ("elopement risk" it says right after the "domestic abuse victim" part on my admission form and psychiatric evaluation). Don't ask me why—I just am. Like right now—if I saw my dad walking up the sidewalk and about to come in, I wouldn't even look to see if he'd been drinking. I'd be out that back patio door before he even knew I was here.

Four

Thursday was a little different. Everybody was still buzzing about Sue Anne and talking about the funeral arrangements and who was going to go. "Mallory's Funeral Home at 2336 Kirby Drive—" Nealon said over the P.A. system. "—At four P.M. tomorrow. All those wishing to pay their last respects may do so at this funeral service." We were in homeroom and Felicia Peters asked what the difference was between a funeral and a memorial service.

"A funeral or wake is when the body is there to be viewed," Ms. Wilkerson said. "And a memorial service is when it is not, often because it was cremated." That seemed pretty reasonable, so we bought it. Almost everybody in the class said they would go, but I bet less than half of them show up. I didn't even know if I wanted to go. It kind of seemed like the right thing to do, but somehow it was all wrong, like I said. I thought I'd talk to Tommy about it in his car at lunch, but about an hour later Mrs. Shamlian asked me to talk to the detective again at lunch. I said okay, but that was before I found out I was seventh and last in line to do it. So I sat there in the office eating my lunch and the other six just sat there and talked and ate, too—but we couldn't talk about Sue Anne or anything about all that. Those were the orders of the detective and since Nealon's door was open nearby and the detective was just down the hall, we just sat there, mostly. I figured he had us do that because he didn't want us changing parts of our stories or descriptions to fit in with what other people had to say. Those detectives are pretty smart.

But get this—it was a different detective. A young guy that looked like he was just out of college. Just as serious, but he didn't look me in the eye as much. He asked some of the same questions plus he asked me to give a whole description in my own words of the situation—the sights, sounds, smells, temperature, the people still around—everything I could think of, he wanted to hear. I thought hard, but I had to tell him that I just looked at her. That's all I really did. The guy looked kind of preppy and professional at the same time. In about fifteen minutes he let me go. "If you remember anything else later, you can contact me through Mrs. Shamlian." He even sounded like one of those college guys.

That afternoon things started to settle down—or maybe it was just me, I'm not sure. Things like that just don't last very long. People get their kicks, start their rumors and then they lose interest.

After school, Tommy and I were able to beat the rush out of the parking lot and we went over to P.B.'s—"Home of the Urge Burger." I had the urge and I had a little money, and I sure didn't feel like going back to that empty apartment. While we sat there in the Dodge, I told him what I thought and then I asked him what he made of the whole thing now.

"Sure—they think we're all stupid. Like we don't know they suspect murder." The word hung in the air as he dangled a french fry in his fingers. "I say let them think whatever they want—it's less trouble that way." I didn't say anything for a while and then he said, "I mean, dead is dead, right? What difference does it make how she died?"

I usually agree with Tommy, but not this time. "Jeez, Tommy, don't you think it matters? If she jumped, it's one thing, but if she was pushed over or thrown off, that's different—that's homicide! Murder's not a game, y'know!"

He gave me that calm look through his glasses and shrugged. "Dead is dead."

Tommy was really something. He didn't think a possible murder was a big deal. Maybe he was trying to convince himself—and me too, if he could. He shook his head slowly and looked off. He wanted to talk about other things—like photography, or scoping out the babes, or maybe he just wanted to finish his burger, fries and shake. Tommy was one of the few unclassified characters at the school. No matter what you tried to pin on him, it didn't stick. He was pretty smart, but quiet, and he didn't care about grades. He wasn't a geek or a mental, or a druggie or runner. He really knew a lot of stuff, too. When I asked him last year why he went to Leary instead of Lamar, he said because it was easier at Leary. That, and the fact that we both agreed that the Lamar students were stuck-up jerks and mall-walkers that none of us wanted to be like.

He didn't have any girlfriends and didn't go out much. He had his own car, but he didn't make as big a deal out of that as he did his cameras. Usually, he just wanted to be left alone. He was content to let people think whatever they wanted to think. Sometimes I thought like he did—if you just stayed quiet, people would leave you alone. I didn't know where he lived for a long time, but then when I asked him, he took me over to his place. It was a pretty nice trailer in the Terrace Plains Trailer Park off Wilcrest Road. Some of the other trailers were rundown-looking, but he kept his looking nice. His dad was in the northwest part of the country working on a forestry project for the government and his mom had died years ago. His dad sent him money every once in a while and to Leary for tuition. The only problem was that Tommy didn't have a phone—said he didn't need one.

His dog, Little Bear, was his real prize. It didn't look so special—like a terrier mutt, but he loved to play with him and take care of him. With his own car and a little money, he could do whatever he wanted. A neat setup. On his living room wall (it seemed cramped in there, no matter where you stood) he had a big oil painting of the prairie and some tiny horses and riders crossing it. It was pretty cool. He liked the old west—cowboys, Indians, relics and stuff like that. I saw that he had books about that stuff on the shelves. He said something once about having some Indian blood in him.

Now, at the burger stand, he looked around as he wiped his mouth with a napkin. I'd already finished my food and was sipping on my Coke. I'd satisfied my "urge" with that sloppy mess of onion, mustard, mayo, lettuce, tomato and one third pound of ground meat. Tommy ate a little slower and I could tell by watching him that he was putting the whole Sue Anne matter behind him. Somehow, it was locked into perspective beneath that straight black hair and black eyes behind the glasses. I wish I could do it that easily. He looked over in the back seat at some of his camera stuff and reached for it and put some of the film rolls back into his camera case. He was always fooling around with that stuff.

Then it dawned on me that his attitude toward the whole

Sue Anne thing was the same one I'd had going through my head the last couple of days. Dead is dead. Right. That really doesn't tell you a lot. It didn't matter that much to Tommy because he didn't see her dead. I did, but I still developed his attitude—maybe I just wanted to ignore it—deny it ever happened. I'm not sure what it all means, but I do know this: Nobody had the right to do that to her. I also know that the image of her on the sidewalk was mighty hard to get out of my head. It was horrible and important somehow—and it should matter. Something should change because of it.

I watched a car full of Leary students go by on Kirby— Terri Druso, Hailey Colthart and that bunch. They were the medium pretty babes in our class. I looked around P.B.'s and everything was still the same. It was the same at the school and the same at home. A girl checks out for good at Leary, but nothing changes. Everything is still the same. It's weird. Maybe it wasn't that important. Maybe none of us is that important. In a week or so, I bet they'll be making jokes about Sue Anne at school. No kidding.

"You didn't get any pictures of it—I mean, of the site or anything?"

"What for? You think anybody'll want to see the spot where Sue Anne hit the sidewalk at fifty miles an hour?" He didn't even look at me as he said it.

"Naw, I guess not—except maybe Ferrito…" That got us both laughing. He practically spit up a french fry before he spoke.

"I'm sure the cops got their photos—but they don't let those out, I hear. You gotta be sick to want to see those." He looked over at me, tapping the steering wheel rhythmically to the music. "Mrs. Howard probably didn't even go over and look when you told her, did she?"

"I don't know—I doubt it. She probably went straight to call the ambulance."

"So you're probably the only one at the school who saw

her lying there dead. What did it look like—did you start to freak, or what?"

I didn't mind talking about it with Tommy, so I told him everything—the walk down the sidewalk, the usual sights, the sound of a car horn somewhere in the distance just before I saw her. And I told him how it made me feel, seeing her face all smashed and the cracks in the concrete. Her legs were all exposed and twisted and helpless. I described the little puddle of blood and the bit of grass sticking up next to her head in the line between the sidewalk sections. And there were some black feathers around her head—like she'd landed on a blackbird or something. It was funny. Now that I was talking to Tommy, I could picture it more clearly. Everything around me as I stood and looked—there was some paper trash blown up against the brick wall of the tower and I remember feeling a chill. I kept talking about it and then about whether I wanted to go to the funeral or not, and then I noticed Tommy. His expression had changed. He just looked at me like I'd said something unbelievable.

"What're you lookin' at? It's just a funeral. You don't have to go if you don't want to. Wilkerson said the body might not even..."

But he just stayed quiet and stared off. I couldn't figure it. I asked him what was wrong but he couldn't hear me—like he was a druggie on something. When he finally snapped back, he pulled his lips into his mouth real tight and started up the car, having to try the key several times before it caught.

"What do you think happened, Wick? Really—do you think she was pushed or did she jump?" He was serious now.

"It's like I said—I don't know. I don't know if anybody will ever know."

"You want to find out?" He had this intense look on his face—kind of wild, but under control. I'd never seen that look on his face before.

"Sure, why not? Lead on, Sherlock."

Five

When we got back to the school it was pretty desolate. A few kids were still hanging around and Vice Principal Patton and Ms. Wilkerson were getting into his car together to go home. He usually gave her a ride to and from school. Tommy put a camera in his jacket and we walked into the school and out the administration hall to the Bronston Tower.

Nobody was around when we got to the stairwell. He looked at the new padlock on the door and glanced around. Nowadays the floor of the tower was pretty much used for storage and was usually unlocked. There were some old cinder blocks and iron bars for concrete reinforcement stacked in the corner from last summer when they were putting up the new deck outside the annex building. Tommy was really something—he just walked over, took an iron bar, came back with it and with two quick jerks he'd pried off the new lock. He just pulled down the yellow police line across the door and opened it.

Once inside, there were a whole lot of steps to go up—five stories worth, and it was dark. There was nothing to do but keep climbing and listening to the echo of our feet on the old stone steps. I was puffing when we finally got to the observation deck area—it had ornamental grating across the open viewing areas. That's as far as anybody really goes, but there was a roof above us and he saw the little hatch door at the top of a few more steps on the other side of the tower. He tried it—he turned the handle and it swung open with a creak. We stepped up onto the tar and gravel floor of the roof.

It was windy and cool up there. We were high above everything now. He stepped over to the ledge where Sue Anne had to have stood. I stood back a ways—I'm not so great with heights.

He stood there holding onto the stone parapet and looking down—he motioned me over. I took one more step. There were a few bricks loose near the edge, but it didn't really look disturbed, just old. I took one more small step, but not too close to him. He was acting a little weird and I didn't feel like playing any games this high up. But the height didn't bother him a bit.

We both looked around and everything looked clean and simple—nothing unusual. I figured there would be some signs that the police had been up there. Nothing. I still didn't look over the edge, but I knew that they hadn't painted any chalk outline where Sue Anne had hit. I guess it was because nobody wanted to freak the students out.

Then he got down on his knees and looked down and around himself on the roof. I don't know why, but I was starting to get scared now—I felt that tightness in my chest. I just got down on my knees too, a few feet behind him, and waited.

"Why do you think she came up here?" He sounded like he was talking to himself.

"I don't know. I didn't think about it—I guess I figured it like everybody else. She came up here because she was going to jump over the edge. But if she wasn't…"

He wasn't listening now. Sure, it changed things if she got pushed. Why would she come up here? Did she get lured up here somehow? He pulled out his camera and aimed it down to take a shot of the concrete below, but then he lowered it without snapping. He looked down for a moment longer and then just turned and came over, sitting down next to me.

"Nobody saw her go to the tower or fall. She was dead when you saw her and you saw her first. You called Mrs. Howard and she kept everyone away and sent you home out the front of the school."

"Yeah—that's right." I couldn't believe he remembered it all so perfectly. I didn't even think he'd been listening to me.

"Who else was around the school then?"

"A few sophomores and juniors from the tutorial—Hailey Colthart, Shelley Prescott, Patti Ranc and a few others."

"Were they the ones in line to talk to that new detective today?"

"Yeah, a couple of them were, come to think of it. It makes sense—those weren't friends of Sue Anne, so they probably had to talk to the detective because they were still around when she died."

He kept nodding slowly and took off his glasses and rubbed one eye. He put the glasses back on and looked at me as he spoke.

"And what were you doing still at the school?"

"Me? Wh—I—I was at the tutorial, you know." I was so

surprised that I didn't know what to say. "What're you talking about? You don't think I—"

"You said you'd been late to a few classes so you had to go to mandatory tutorial, right?"

"Right—like I said—"

He was grinning a bit now, back to his old self—a little amused that he'd gotten to me with his questions. Then he started thinking hard, wondering aloud about it all.

"It's hard to tell what happened. Somebody could've waited up here for her—if he could get her up here somehow."

We both looked out and around us at the surrounding streets, cars and trees of Kirby Drive. Off in the distance, the downtown part of the city looked hazy in the afternoon air. The big, glassy buildings stuck up starkly in a cluster from the ground. The setting sun reflected in the glass and made them pillars of fire—they'd be like that for the next hour or so.

"Jeez, unless you just liked the view, I don't know why anybody'd come up here. But don't forget—" I added, in a pretty smart way, for me, "—it could've been one of her girlfriends who did it. They can shove somebody just as good as a guy can."

He nodded in agreement. The wind picked up and threw our hair around. Once the fear left, it kind of gave me a sense of power to be up here. Like I was on top of the world and I could really do something important if I wanted to. Then I heard it again—the music of the ice cream truck. Only now, the same melody drifted up to us gently from far away, and I could see a few kids running off way down Windemere to catch up to it. It had already come and gone from the apartment and I was glad I wouldn't have to listen to it blaring out right in front of me. After that stop, it made its way over to Windemere and to Leary, and then on down the street to where it was right now.

"Listen—" I said, "Do you think..." He cocked his head like he was listening to me, but I could tell he was thinking about something else. "Do you think somebody could've just done it for a kick—to find out what it would feel like to kill somebody? I mean, like a thrill kill—"

Then he did something weird—like he was suddenly alone. He looked off slowly into the sun, his hands open in front of him, and when he brought his eyes back down he had changed somehow. Now he looked like he was ready to attack or something. It was freaky, because he was breathing hard when he spoke.

"No, it was not just for a thrill." He started breathing more like normal, and then he took his glasses off and held them. "My father once told me that life is like floating down the river seated backward on a raft—your eyes watch the water you have just come through. You have your back to the future. This is how the wise and brave man lives. The coward looks to the front but he cannot bear to see the future."

We just sat there for a while. I didn't know what to do.

Six

"Is everything all right, Wick?"

"Sure—I guess so."

"No problems?"

"Naw."

"Are you through with the casseroles yet? I bet you're tired of them by now."

"They're okay."

"Are you packing your lunch every day? A good lunch? With that deli meat I bought?"

"Yep—every day."

"How's the schoolwork coming?"

"Okay—got a history project due."

"Oh, have you started it yet?"

"Yeah, but things at school are a little different now."

"What's different?"

"Uh, not much—I just mean the students and all—spring fever, I guess."

I heard a couple of men talking behind her and she said something to them. She sounded a little rushed.

"All right, Wick, we can talk a little later. I'm glad things are going so well. I wish I could be there with you—but it looks like I may have to spend more time here. You understand, don't you?"

"Uh-huh."

"Okay, I've got to go now. Call me if you need to—and be good."

"I will. Bye, Mom."

"Bye, bye. I love you."

She hung up and I did too. At least she was where there were people. She probably didn't want to hear about all the weird stuff at school. It would just set her off. I looked around myself. Sometimes in this apartment I felt like I was being punished—punished by having to be alone, like I'm not fit to be around other people because of something I did. I know it's stupid, but I feel that way sometimes. Maybe I'm just bored.

I walked to school the next day. Tommy usually picked me up, but he had to go in early to develop some pictures in the darkroom. I got there a little late and when I went to the office to see if I could get a pass for homeroom, I smelled it. The people in the office did, too. It really stunk—and then we saw the black smoke rolling toward us under the ceiling of the administration hall.

Nealon rushed out and in less than a minute we were all standing around the janitor's room which was pouring out that black smoke and crackling with little sparks. Mendoza, the janitor, was spraying it with the extinguisher and Patton was trotting up with another one.

I was going to stay and watch, but Nealon started telling everybody to get back to their first period class and stay there, so I went on. Patton never noticed me. As I passed Mendoza I saw that he had burned his face a little and his hair was singed. He wasn't too bright and Nealon knew it, so he took the extinguisher from the stocky little Mexican guy and sprayed it in there along with Patton.

It was kind of funny—Mendoza was looking around with this helpless look on his face, wanting somebody to tell him what to do. He was worried something pathetic—probably because he was afraid he'd lose his job over it. He had his palms behind him up against the wall and his feet were sliding around on the floor where that foamy extinguisher stuff had leaked out.

Well, the whole school smelled on account of it, so for the second period everybody just stood around outside and talked. Tommy went back inside to take some photos of it for the school newspaper—they'd probably let him do it. The fire was put out pretty quickly. Then I heard a few guys talking and heard King's name. King was nowhere around and people just naturally assumed he had something to do with it. I don't know if arson is included in his "repertoire"—as Patton called King's discipline record ("rap sheet" everybody else called it). As I looked around, I saw him over by the administration hall exit. He was over there near Mendoza, who was still coughing and trying to clear his eyes of the smoke. I saw Mendoza walk in his funny way out to his old, green pickup truck and I watched King just walk right past Patton with a smile on his face. In a little while he was standing among the guys and laughing, his twin mirrors gleaming as they reflected the sun. Around him they talked in low voices and sort of kicked at the ground. King, a head taller than most, just had that look of satisfaction on his face as he looked over the crowd.

The teachers stood around and talked among themselves, too. We heard that the fire hadn't spread and that it would be safe to go in after a while. It would be okay if we just kept the windows open. For some weird reason Ferrito was standing near the teachers and laughing—he must've thought it was just hilarious. I'm telling you, he is one sick dude. He moved in a kind of jumpy way over toward King and the gang and I could see the girls watching him. They like him. Why? That's what I want to know.

In a few minutes Tommy came out. He stopped to take one photo of all of us standing out in the courtyard and then came up to me.

"Everything okay in there?"

"Yeah, but it'll stink for the rest of the day, I'll bet." He said it matter-of-factlike—his mind was on something else. The excitement was over—everything but finding out what or who caused it. Nealon was waving his arms for us to go back inside.

Tommy zipped up his camera stuff and we went back on in. We'd had a few false alarms this year—somebody thought it was real cute to set off the alarm and get everybody out of class. I figured that once Nealon saw the situation he didn't want anybody to call for the firetrucks because we'd had them out for those false alarms and it made the school look bad. But when you think about it, there really was a fire this time and those of us in the office smelled and saw the smoke before we knew anything else. Great. There's a real fire and the jerky headmaster decides not to call the fire department. Endanger all our lives, why don't you?

The stinking day went on, and I felt like walking right out of that place—like a protest, because no firetruck showed up. When we were driving home later, I told Tommy about it and he agreed, sort of.

"Yeah, you're right—but it was just a little chemical or

electrical fire in the janitor's room—it was out in five minutes. That smelly smoke was the real problem "

"That's not the point. It could've spread. There's people in there—you and me. What if they couldn't put it out with those little extinguishers?"

"But they did." He had that same calm look on his face now. It was useless to keep talking about it. Then we were driving up toward Mallory's Funeral Home and we saw some of the students from Leary going in. Tommy slowed down.

"Do you want to go in?" I asked.

He just shook his head slowly. He looked at me to see if I wanted to go in there for the service, but I motioned for him to go on. It would be some priest or minister and all you'd hear is the girls crying and saying how much they'll miss her— when they probably cut her down so bad behind her back that when she found out she jumped off the tower. Or maybe one of them actually pushed her over the edge. Who knows? Yeah, maybe someone's in there sniffling and carrying on because nobody would suspect you if you went in there and listened to the priest and cried a lot. Anyway, I was definitely not in the mood for it.

When Tommy let me out at the apartment he reached over onto the back seat as he lifted a hand goodbye. I told him I'd see him later and I happened to turn and see him through the back passenger-side window—I noticed him putting another roll of film into his carrying case. Up popped something odd from under the zipper. It was a black feather.

Seven

So a whole week goes by and everything's still the same. Everybody stopped talking about Sue Anne and nobody knew a thing about the fire, except everybody figured that one of the guys set it and that King was somehow behind it. Nobody stepped forward and said who did it. We were one week closer to summer and I had no idea what I was going to do during those three months. How do you get a summer job without a car?

One other thing happened. We got to school on Thursday and right there on the front side of the tower, facing the road—right there in big, white, spray-painted letters was this:

Whatever Happened at Leary High?

It was those damn mall-walkers from Lamar. They put up a ladder and wrote that up there in the middle of the night. They'd read about it in the paper—the death of Sue Anne Chadwick was being investigated further by the homicide department because of possible "foul play." Then the fire in the janitor's room—somebody here at Leary probably told them about that, too. So those wise guys figured they'd let us know they were better than us by defacing our school. Jerks. And who knew how long it would be before Mendoza got up there to wash it off?

I had another session with my psychologist, Billy Stephens. He always said, "Call me Billy," so I did. He was a good guy. It was a little different this time—he wanted to know how I was doing after the whole Sue Anne thing. We talked about death. Actually, it was more talk about living up until you die.

He said neat things—like when he talked about invisible doors. He said that all important doors in life are invisible, and usually we don't know one is there until we pass through it. And he said Sue Anne had just passed through one of the doors. He said that he'd gone through these doors in his life and he felt that I was about to go through one, too. I asked him how he could tell and he said he couldn't really explain how he knew—he just knew.

And listen to this—I know that he'd had sessions with Sue Anne too, but not because he'd told me. When I asked him if he thought it was even possible that Sue Anne jumped, he said "No." I mean, he said it like I'd asked him what time it was and he said "Two-thirty." He said that the police were investigating the incident because it was probably a homicide. The faculty and staff had been questioned before they talked with any students. He knew a lot more than what was said in the two little articles in the newspaper and he said he thought I should know what was really happening because I was involved. That was pretty decent of him.

It was better with Billy this time. Not the usual topics and questions. I mean, he didn't just ask—have you felt like running away again? How much time do you spend alone at home? Have you seen your father? Was he drunk? Did he try to hit you?

He let me talk a while and tell him what was on my mind, but I knew he had to get some information from me. He worked for the M.H.M.R.A.—the state Mental Health and Mental Retardation Association—as a staff psychologist on call at Leary. There was nothing to worry about with him. He was older—fifty-five he'd said once, and he started studying to be a psychologist because he liked it—said that he'd been a stockbroker for a long time and that he'd kill himself—actually blow his brains out if he kept doing that stuff. Said it was worth it to him to make a lot less money and still be sane. Somehow, I trusted this guy. He looked like he didn't have a wife or anything. Dressed kind of sloppy, like he was in a hurry to get out of the house in the morning—but he didn't rush you out the door after fifty minutes when your time was up. If you had something to say, he'd listen.

He was real bald and smoked a pipe. And he looked sad today, and tired—maybe over Sue Anne, I don't know. But he said something else. I'd never heard it before. He said that parents and teachers, principals and coaches—none of them knew how to discipline their kids anymore. He said they were all afraid to do it. Afraid that if they punished a kid or embarrassed him that he'd jump off a building or run away or start doing drugs to get even. So they stopped trying to punish them even when they needed it. He asked me what I thought about that. I didn't have much of a response. Then he told me that sometimes he thought that some of the Leary students who nobody could punish no matter what they did, came to sessions with him and they felt like that was their punishment. First, I thought he was making a joke, but then I didn't think so. Later, I wondered if he was trying to tell me that I was one of those kids who thought that.

I left thinking it over. The only punishment I felt I got was being bored and lonely. Tommy, my best friend, was acting weird now and—*no, no, no, no!* I wasn't thinking about running away again. I mean, these shrinks—it's like they think we're running to be cool or just to rebel—or because there's some great place faraway. Some of them, like Billy, know we're just running away from something—a lot of things, maybe. But right now, I don't have anything to run away from. Nobody's home. It's like the place is all mine and it still doesn't matter to me.

Mom came into town for a day, packed again and left for another week. It's not her fault.

eight

Outside of homeroom the next morning, I had just shut my locker and spun the combination lock when I turned and saw Shelley Prescott walking right up to me—Shelley herself. But she had a confused look on her face as she looked at the room I'd just walked out of.

"Oh, hi—you're Wick—"

A pause. Her confused look fell on me now. I just looked at her and swallowed some air. It was really her and she was talking to me. Speak, you idiot.

"Uh, yeah—that's me—"

"God, is this it? No—" She clutched her geometry book to her chest and squinted as she looked over at the door again.

45

Maybe there were numbers up there a few decades ago.

"What're you looking for, Shelley?" I figured I should ask since there was nothing to see on or above the door now.

"I've got to go to a French Club meeting sixth period—in Room A 111." She looked around again and I looked at the little polo player on her baby-blue shirt—and then down. She had those smooth, tanned legs that thickened and disappeared up under her gray plaid skirt.

"None of these rooms have numbers," she said. "How're you supposed to know?" She hunched her shoulders and crinkled up her nose as she stepped closer to me. Talk, Wick. Don't stare at her.

"Well, uh—this one's A 116. I know because it's homeroom—for me, I mean—" My mouth had gone dry. "And this is the last one in the hall. So, I guess 111's at the other end—" I pointed. Right. As if she didn't know where the other end of the hall was.

"You're one of the guys who was in tutorials when I was, right?" She flashed a smile and I smiled back. God, she was pretty.

"Yeah—" We just stood there and looked at each other for a moment. I knew I was late for class again—so was she. But it didn't seem to bother her.

"You speak French?" It was the best that I could come up with. I swallowed hard, trying to wet my mouth again.

"Oui—un petit peu," she said, exaggerating the French accent and playfully throwing back her head, the polo player bulging out at me. "That mean's 'yes, a little bit'—but not that much." She laughed a little and I was about to laugh with her when Kendall Wright, a senior, walked up behind me, moving fast.

"Hi, Missy. You're late for class again." He just kept walking past us with a grin on his face as he looked down at his wristwatch and shook his head. I mean, he did it like he wasn't late himself, like he was in charge of attendance.

"Oh, shush!" she blurted out teasingly. She looked back at me but I could tell she was about to go. Think fast.

"Did he just call you 'Missy'?"

"Oh yeah—everybody here thinks I'm so preppy—you know. I've got a brother in college back East, and I used to go to Lamar. So does that make me preppy?"

"I guess not—" I thought about saying yes to that question, but I didn't want her to get mad at me.

"Right—that's what I mean."

But I could tell she liked the nickname. And it did fit her. She shifted the book to her other hand and looked around the hall. I figured she really didn't care if she made it to the geometry class or not. I didn't have anything else to say, so she spoke up.

"Well, thanks. I'll find it sooner or later. Be nice if there were at least a few room numbers around here, though."

I agreed and she fluttered her fingers in a goodbye and turned to go. I watched her walk down the hall and when she got a couple of doors down, she turned and looked back at me. I was still staring and now she saw me doing it. Great, Wick. I turned and walked off the other way, even though my class was right near where she was walking now. I was short of breath, but I felt great. I'd really talked with her.

Get this—I talked with her again two days later. That time it wasn't so bad, talking about a few of the teachers and the school as a whole. She told me a little about herself when I asked—said her parents go out of the country a lot. She told me that she lived in the Memorial area of the city, and when I said that was a great place to live, she even said I could go and visit her there sometime if I was in the area. I couldn't tell if she really meant it or not. I didn't have a single class with her but I thought about her a lot—and when I saw her in the halls or after school, I really wondered what it would be like to kiss her.

When I asked her why she came to Leary, she said it was because her grades had gone down at Lamar. I thought about that—Lamar. Great. A mall-walker decides to come over to Hell High. I didn't tell her that, of course. I noticed Smeg and Kendall Wright hanging around her too, and looking at me when I talked to her. I just talked for a couple of minutes and then we went our separate ways. I told her I might call her sometime and it seemed okay with her. It made me feel great, even with classes just going on and on, with the same old faces and the same old laziness and boredom of the students.

And Tommy. Man, I don't know what to do there. He said he couldn't pick me up for school in the morning anymore, even though we had an agreement about that. I'd always paid for some of his gas. And he's been taking off from school early, even cutting some classes to go. He was real interested in the Sue Anne thing for a while, and now, nothing. When I sat next to him in class, he just kind of shrugged and had nothing to say—only that he had to think about things.

We had a discussion about race and ethnic stuff in Jenkins' class and it was one of the rare times Tommy spoke up. He said, "everybody comes from somewhere—you can't help where you come from or who you are."

But he hardly got the words out of his mouth before Jenkins cut him off and said—"That's true, but we can help what we will become. No one's ethnic or racial background has to be a limitation in our society. That's one of the good things about America." God, I thought he was going to start singing the national anthem or something. When I looked at Tommy I saw him shaking his head. Jenkins didn't get the point he was making. I figured Tommy was looking at the past—there's a time to do that, too. It's not just always looking at the future—planning, positive thinking, hard work and all that stuff.

Then Jamaal Jefferson, the only black student in the class, said that blacks will never be free until America has a black president and blacks were running the major corporations. Got real huffy about it. The discussion went nowhere from there—especially after Jenkins said that high positions like those had to be earned, not handed out on the basis of race or ethnic origin. The last thing Tommy said was that he'd always heard that it was your past that tells you who you are, not your future. He said, "White people always think the future is theirs, so they love to think about it." But Jamaal had already blown the whole thing off by then. I heard Tommy a little differently this time. It was like he didn't really include himself when he talked about white people. I never asked him much about his background. He was kind of private about things—some people were like that at Leary, and you didn't hear much of their stories. I mean, with most people you usually heard about why they wound up at Leary and a lot of times you heard more than you wanted to hear—and like I said, the stories aren't so pretty.

Like the ones who tried to kill themselves, or the druggies, or the ones that got beat up at home. Sure, I'd gotten knocked around a few times when my dad was drunk, but it wasn't every day like some. And other stuff—like DeFranco sleeping in his car for a week when his old lady just left town after they had to leave their apartment—he didn't have anyplace to stay, but wouldn't admit it and stay with one of the guys. Patton had asked him why he was the first one in school every day that week, and how he'd caught that bad cold. It was cold outside, that's why. We knew about it—but we didn't tell. I mean, it was like a code among us. Why hurt the guy more?

And some of us aren't all that proud of where we come from and who we are. Like Zingale—his old man is in the state pen for armed robbery. Zing's on the full state program at Leary—no tuition. We all know it. What's Zing supposed to do about it? And some of the guys had been dealing drugs for two or three years before they got caught and eventually sent here. They might just turn on you like a hurt animal if you up and asked them a bunch of personal questions. Or they might just say—"What's it to ya?" get mad and maybe try to mess you up. I mean, King and those guys might punch you in the chest and cave in your rib cage.

Some of us were better off—like Janine Barrow, Kirk Patrikis, Penny Newall, Kendall Wright and probably Shelley Prescott. The way they dressed and acted and the stuff they talked about—like Janine was always talking about their trips to Europe and the Cayman Islands. Sometimes Shelley sounds like that. Her folks had money, that's for sure. Maybe her parents are weird and nobody knows it—but I doubt it.

Nine

The next day Tommy finally felt like doing something, so we decided to go out Highway 59 to a place called Tio's—a Mexican restaurant he liked. But he didn't have any money, so I told him I'd treat if it wasn't too expensive. It was cool with him. We went over to his place first so he could feed his dog.

We got off the Fannin exit of 59 and went past a few strip shopping centers and a new low-cost housing development called Windwood. Just off Wilcrest Road we reached the Terrace Plains Trailer Park. It didn't look as good to me as it had earlier. Some little Mexican kids were chasing around between the trailers playing hide-and-seek and there were two overturned garbage cans near the entrance. He pulled up to his trailer and as we got out he took his camera stuff with him. He trotted on up the steps and I followed a ways behind him, looking over at the side of the trailer. A little Mexican girl looked up at me with her twinkling, big, dark eyes. She was dressed in a little white dress with red and yellow flower patterns sewn on it. Barefoot—she had wet her hands on the slick wall and was standing in the big puddle beneath it. She ran off, gurgling and laughing.

I stepped inside with Tommy and he set his camera stuff on the coffee table in the living room. I expected Little Bear to come running up to him but he didn't, and we turned and listened to a low roaring sound coming from the far side of the place. As we went over, it sounded to me like water was running somewhere.

I was right behind him a few feet when it happened—he opened the bathroom door and a huge five-foot wall of water knocked us over onto the floor and back across to the kitchen. Frantically, I pulled myself up out of the water as it sank immediately, flooding the whole trailer. I turned and tried to help Tommy up and he started coughing real bad—he'd swallowed a lot of water.

I just held him up—both of us up—against the wall to catch our breath. It was some kind of nightmare. We just listened to the water still rushing out of the faucets in the bathroom. When we got our breath, I went in and turned all the spigots off. Tommy still had his face pressed against the wall in disbelief when I came back to him.

"We'll be all right, Tommy—God, I'm sorry..." But he was in shock. Then I looked down and saw what had happened. Up against the adjoining wall Little Bear was lying out flat—dead—drowned. Tommy just looked down at him and I thought he was going to crumble. He went over, knelt down and turned him over gently. The little dog's eyes were rolled back and his fur was all wet, teeth clenched.

Tommy just started crying—great, heaving sobs that shook his body. He stroked the slick fur softly and stared around helplessly. I edged away, not knowing what to do. I could feel it inside me. My chest was tight and I was gasping for breath—soaked all the way down into my water-filled sneakers. I had to get out of there—run away. Now—fast.

"Don't go, please—I…" He looked at me and then at Little Bear again and he bent forward, his shoulders jerking as he wept loudly.

"Tommy—we can—I mean, if you want, we can bury him. The place'll dry out—" But he didn't hear me.

I walked over and looked back inside the bathroom. All around the edges of the door and the floorboards were thick gobs of axle grease. No water could get out, except through the window which was opened just a crack on the far wall next to the toilet. The bathtub was still full and I pulled up the stopper to let the water out and I watched several black feathers bob and float on top of the water, then get sucked toward the drain.

He came up behind me, holding one hand against the wall and looking into the tub. He reached down and picked up one of the feathers. I felt cold now from my wet clothes and he was white—as white as the porcelain tub. I looked back at the door jambs and the barely opened window. You don't have to be a detective to figure out what had happened.

I guided us back out to the living room but he kept walking until he got back outside—the trailer looked like a hurricane had come through it. A lot of his stuff was ruined. We sat down on the steps leading up to the trailer. His black hair was slicked down against his skull and his glasses had been knocked off. He still held the black feather in his hand. I was shivering from the cold now.

"Tommy, let's go to my place—or somewhere. We gotta

change clothes or we'll catch pneumonia."

But he just sat there, holding the feather like it was some kind of poison dart and staring at it.

"C'mon, man!" I was about to jerk him up out of his trance and make him tell me what the deal was with the feathers. But then he spoke.

"By the air—
By the fire—
By the water—
By the earth…"

I had no idea what he meant. He just looked so spooked and helpless. His old shirt and jeans leaked onto the steps. He looked at me now—really looked at me like he never had before.

"Wick—I need help. Will you help me?"

Part Two

THE AMERICAN INDIAN RESURVATION

In the United States, the American Indian resurvation is an area set aside by the fediral or statte government for the use of Indians. America has aproximately 285 fediral and statte Indian resurvations which cover more that 50 million acres in about 30 states. about 1,100,000 approximately American Indians live in the United Stattes almost one-half of them make their homes on a resurvation of some kind.

Indian resurvations are usu ally owned by the

Indians and are held in trust for them by the fediral or statte governments. The Bureau of Indian afairs, a agency of the Dept. of Interior, manages most of the fediral progroms on resurvations.

Many Indians prefer to live on resurvations so they can practice and perserve the tribal customs and old ways of lives. Some resurvations are owned by an entire tribe and others are divided into individual or large tribal plots and passed down from fathers to sons old generations. Some indians work in sawmills and businesses which belong to the Tribe others may have jobs in nearby factorys or mines owned by white people. The U.S. has many Indian resurvations but mostly they are west of the Missisippi River...

It went on like that. Tommy's research paper didn't look so hot—like he just copied most of it out of the encyclopedia. Jenkins wasn't all that impressed either, since he only gave him a C-minus. He'd assigned eight to ten pages and Tommy gave him five.

The rest of his paper talked about Indian lifestyles and customs and every once in a while he included a big phrase like "The Snyder Act of 1921," "The Indian Citizenship Act," "The Johnson O'Malley Act," or the "Termination Policy." Sounded to me like he just dropped those in there so Jenkins would think he did some research. He started in a little bit on how the Indians have been cheated and all—but there were so many mistakes in spelling and grammar that some of it didn't make much sense. And there really wasn't any conclusion to the thing. It just stopped with the words—"...and modern day Indians like the Keowahk must honor their fathers in the land of their fathers." Period. No footnotes or bibliography. I thought Jenkins would have a cow about that, but this was all he said:

> TOMMY—This is not a bad effort. You must discipline yourself to stick to your topic, though— "American Indian Reservations." The rest, regardless of your personal interest or involvement, must remain peripheral. Where are the footnotes and bibliography? Clean up your many errors in punctuation, grammar and spelling. Indent for new paragraphs. Proofread carefully.
>
> By the way, I tried to look up the Keowahk Indians and couldn't find out much at all about them. Are they still a viable, distinct tribe?

I thought Tommy got off pretty easy because I had nine pages on the Battle of Gettysburg and not all that many errors and he gave me a B-minus. We'd just gotten out of Jenkins' class an hour ago and we looked over each other's paper in study hall. After that he had geometry and I went on to English class. I thought about it—him and the Indian stuff. He was part Keowahk Indian, but he never talked about it. I was surprised that he chose it for his topic for the history research project. He never said anything about himself in the paper (Jenkins would take you down a whole letter grade if you used first person)—but you could tell he was one. I mean, if you knew him. Maybe Jenkins knows—he probably does. Tommy said something in the paper about becoming a man— becoming a brave. But none of it really made good sense to me until I talked to him later that afternoon.

"I don't know, man—" Tommy said, looking straight ahead, watching the other cars lined up in front of him trying to get out of the parking lot after school. He'd backed into his spot that morning and we just sat there, neither one of us in a hurry, waiting for the rush to die down before he started up the car to leave.

"I don't know either," I said. "I don't know why people can't just leave each other alone." I watched him to see if he was really listening and I couldn't tell. He was and he wasn't. He was in that weird kind of mood again. Quiet, but thinking in a far-off way.

"I guess everybody gets tested," he said. "If you're going to be brave, you've got to be tested—by the air, fire, water, and earth…"

"What?" But as soon as I said it, I remembered that it was the same phrase he used when we sat there on the steps of his trailer, soaking wet.

"It's what the Keowahk tribesmen believe." He pronounced "Keowahk" kind of funny. "It's a choice of honor or shame, and passing the tests is the only way to escape the shame and prove yourself worthy."

We sat there and watched an anxious father trying to back out of a parking place and get out fast, but it didn't look like there was enough room for the maneuver. Tommy turned on the radio and one of the familiar top-forty tunes played softly. This time he didn't keep beat against the outside of his car door like he usually does.

Then I started thinking and I figured something out. The things that were happening weren't just accidents or pranks. Sue Anne Chadwick was pushed from the tower roof, falling through the air onto the sidewalk. The fire in the school was next, and then the water which flooded Tommy's place. The air, the fire, the water—now the only thing left was the earth, and I couldn't figure that one out. Maybe something else was going to happen.

I mentioned it and he just nodded and stared off. It was like he didn't know what to say—and I couldn't tell how much he knew. But he had one of the black feathers next to him on the seat of his car. He turned up the music but as soon as he did it, the music got drowned out by the ice cream truck down the street, which was continuing its rounds after leaving my apartment. We watched Shelley and Janine and a few other babes come out to their cars. Sometimes Shelley drove a new green Camaro—really tough looking. We scoped them out pretty good and then King came by and looked right at us before he and Ferrito went over to King's car. Ferrito looked like he was staggering and blasted on something. (So what else is new?) He had blue, green, pink and bright orange colors in his hair. Then they jumped into the bright red Corvette with King laying on that distinctive horn of his. Just to let everyone know that he was ready to go. The 'Vette had a turbo-charged, fuel-injection V-8 engine and when the coast was clear, everybody knew he would blow out of there really cool-like.

A few teachers were pulling out and so was Nealon. Tommy and I just sat there. It was weird about him. If he wanted to talk, he talked. If he didn't want to talk, there was nothing in the world you could do to make him. He was a private kind of guy, all right. I wondered how much was going on in his head and I wondered how smart it was to get hooked up with him. I noticed that he had some of his things— blankets, some clothing, and important papers—all stuffed in his duffel bag in the back seat. That damn ice cream music was real loud again and I told him to get us out of there as soon as possible. He turned the key and there was the same old trouble with the ignition switch again—he had to try it six or seven times before it caught and started.

"Got to get that fixed," he said.

Eleven

Another day went by and I felt like going on over to Tommy's trailer, but then I decided against it. At school, he said he'd been airing his place out but that it was still damp. I told him he could stay with me for a couple of days if he wanted to—Ma's room was empty. I was surprised when he said okay.

He came in that night about ten with his duffel bag and that was it. I showed him Ma's room but he didn't like it—said he'd rather sleep on the floor in my room. It was okay with me. I threw down some sheets, set the alarm and we turned off the lights. It was kind of weird having him there. Maybe he just didn't want to be alone. Maybe I didn't either.

In the darkness our breathing rose and fell and each of us could tell that the other one wasn't falling asleep.

"Wick…"

"Yeah?"

"I got something to say."

"What is it?"

"I got trouble—real trouble."

I couldn't hear him breathe at all now. It was tense. All I could hear was a disembodied voice coming up from the floor, hanging in the air.

"Somebody's trying to get me…"

"You mean…kill you?"

"Yes…or make me do something I don't want to do."

"What don't you want to do?"

"You see—I'm…I'm not like everybody else. I'm a full-blooded Keowahk Indian. My parents raised me on the Cattawaugas reservation until I was eight. My father was like—the chief. I have attended the white man's school for many years now. My mother died eleven years ago and my father died two years ago. It's true that he'd been working in the Northwest on a government forestry project—that's when he died."

He paused and I heard him breathing again as I shifted my weight. The bedsprings jangled underneath me as we both looked up at the ceiling.

"In three days I will be eighteen years old—I must not shame my fathers. I must become a brave."

"How do you do that? I've tried to ask, but you never say anything."

"I know—it's not always best to talk of it. By the air, by the fire, by the water, by the earth—every young man who wants to become a Keowahk brave must face the four trials. In the old days, you had to climb the highest mountain, be branded by hot coals, swim a raging river…"

"Jeez—and what's the last one? By the earth—"

"This no one knows—the great earth spirit alone answers this. Your final trial is the most severe. Many do not survive it."

"But how do they die? Somebody must know."

"Those who know will never tell because it is a sacrilege. Whoever is behind the death of the girl, the fire, and the flooding of my home has now made it clear—I am expected to defend my honor and the honor of my fathers by facing the four trials."

"But why push Sue Anne off the roof? That's no trial for you."

"No, it isn't. He just wanted to strike close to me—at the school I attend. He doesn't want to kill me now. But he's trying to make me…dishonor my fathers by giving over the land which our people still have."

"Huh?"

"When my father died, I became the last heir of the chief's small tribe, possessor of the old Keowahk hunting grounds—our part of the reservation land. It becomes official when I turn eighteen. The land is my possession and responsibility, unless I sign the documents which were mailed to me over a month ago. These papers would turn the land over to a different tribe which is also protected by the U.S. government, under the agreement my people made many years ago. The threats are intended to make me sign the papers, but I will not. I will not give up our sacred land, no matter what may happen to me. If necessary, I will appoint in writing a new chief for my people. It must be a brave man."

"Who mailed you the documents?"

"I don't know. But whoever did it was the one who killed Sue Anne."

"And set the fire and flooded your trailer?"

"Yes. The letter with the documents demands that I make

my decision and return to the reservation before midnight on the day before my birthday."

"What if you don't?"

"He'll probably force me to—or kill me if I don't."

I swallowed hard. "Wh-what are you going to do?"

"I will be brave."

"Jeez, Tommy—don't you think you oughta call the police or something? That's gotta be against the law."

"No—I cannot call for help. It is not against our law. The land is ours only if we can hold it."

"But if it's really yours, legally, why don't you just leave town for a while until after your birthday—where nobody can find you?" There was silence, then—

"He might try to kill me when I returned. No, I must not run away, for running away would dishonor my fathers. I cannot live with that. It is better that I die than be dishonored or give up our sacred land—and that is why I need your help. When I face the final trial it will be best if more than one person knows exactly who is putting me to the test. And we must bring to justice anyone responsible for murdering the girl."

I didn't want him to hear my breathing now—rapid, tight. I was scared. Somebody who had already killed once was after him and now he was right next to me—and his car was parked outside.

"Was everything okay at your trailer?"

"After I buried Little Bear I collected a few things and did not go back there."

"What? Where have you been for two days?"

"In my car, in the malls, and at school. It was not wise to go back home."

The words floated up and I could hardly believe them. It didn't really sound like the Tommy I knew. And I thought I knew this guy. He'd been running for his life and he didn't tell me—didn't tell anyone. The picture of Sue Anne all broken up and bloody flashed through my mind again. Whoever did that set the fire at the school and broke into his trailer and flooded it. He could be waiting outside right now.

We both heard it. The sudden, sharp sound of a door closing outside the window. I bolted upright in bed and before I knew it Tommy was at the window, silently watching from behind a crack in the drapes. He whispered without moving.

"She's gone into the apartment directly across from us. Do you have a blond female neighbor, middle-aged, license BEA 464?"

"Uh, yeah—Mary Rossicky. She stays out late a lot."

In the dull light from the window, I saw the glint of the sharp steel blade in his hand—I hadn't realized that it had been lying next to him on the floor. He came back and sat next to my bed.

"All the doors and windows are locked and bolted, right?"

"Right," I whispered.

My heart still pounded and my head swam with it all—the urgency, the danger—the honor so important to him. And I thought, stupidly, about his research paper that neither Jenkins nor I had bothered to read very closely. Now I was right in the middle of it. Somehow, I found the courage to tell him what I did.

"Tommy—listen, man. You're my friend and I'm going to help you. If you need to stay here, that's okay. If you want me to go out to your reservation with you, I will."

He was silent for just a moment before he said, "Thanks, Wick. I will always be your friend."

And as I look back, I understand what that really meant— yet I wondered why things had to end the way they did. That night, we listened to the soft night sounds outside and the ceiling fan above me as it rotated quietly, slowly stirring the air, making the shadows move hypnotically against the pale ceiling. It was like some dim, fluorescent universe was being projected up there like a movie on a screen. It shimmered and fluttered before my eyes again and again.

Twelve

When the alarm went off it startled me. Tommy was already up and I just laid there, tired. Tired and jumpy. Throughout my morning classes I sat and wrote out the possibilities—who I thought could be involved.

King was a logical guess, with his reputation. I don't quite know how he could've done it, but I knew he'd do anything if it meant money or being cool. The only other people around were Mrs. Howard and the few students from tutorial—all of them except a few of the younger babes had already gone home out the front way. But if it was any one of them, she'd have to be a great actress because I saw the look on each of their faces when they first heard about it.

Maybe Dr. Nealon or Patton were still around. (Now that's a creepy feeling.) The police probably knew a lot from their questioning, but how was I supposed to find out? I couldn't start asking a bunch of questions of Mrs. Shamlian or those detectives—they'd get real suspicious and start pumping me for information again—and I told Tommy I wouldn't let anybody know anything about his stuff.

Whoever it was knew a lot about Tommy's life here at the school—and probably about mine, too. I hated to still think about it, but any one of those giggly freshman or sophomore babes could've pushed her off if she felt like it. She could do it and no one would suspect her whether she went to the funeral and cried or sat back in class and laughed about it all. But it's not so funny when somebody dies—or when somebody you really know, like Tommy, might get killed. He made it sound like it had to be an outsider—from the reservation or something. But there weren't any strangers around before I saw Sue Anne that day. I'd have noticed if there were.

It was time for history class—Tommy would be in there. I stuck the notepaper I was writing on into my pocket to throw away at home.

Jenkins lectured about Mormons and the westward movement. I watched him stand there and explain things as he smoothed down the lapels on his jacket. I thought about the fire in the janitor's room—no big deal. I was there to see who was around for that and Tommy got there later to get some photos, too. The only thing those photos showed was Nealon and Patton and a few black feathers on the floor. Tommy had picked one of them up, like I figured. Then the bathroom stunt in his trailer—the only clue there was all that axle grease. Great. That you can get at any auto parts shop. And if any of those Mexican kids or their parents saw someone going in or out that bathroom window, they might not say—and me and Tommy didn't speak Spanish anyway. I tried to recall if

King was in school that day, but I couldn't. Besides all that, Tommy was staying with me again tonight and he refused to go near his trailer. I don't blame him. Things just looked hopeless. I mean, how could I figure anything out if the detectives couldn't?

Tommy was sitting a couple of seats away from me, and when Jenkins saw his time running out, he finished up his lecture. The bell rang and when we were outside in the hall, we talked for a little while. I told him how hopeless it all seemed.

"Look," he said calmly, "those detectives don't know the answer yet either. When it comes to Sue Anne, you saw it all as near to the time of death as anyone. And you said yourself that you didn't tell the police everything you knew—you just told them what you thought they wanted to know."

I had to agree there. He said that if I wasn't too tired I should just go over the questions the two detectives asked and answer them as fully as I could for our own purposes. Every detail I could remember.

So we split up, Tommy to geometry class and me to English. While we were supposed to be reading some short story by Ray Bradbury, I pulled out the notepaper from my pocket and wrote out all the questions that both detectives asked me. But I still didn't know why some of them were important.

Were you the one who found the body?
Did it move or show any signs of life?
Do you always take that way home?
Why did you go home that way on Tuesday?
Did you know the girl?
How well did you know her?
What was she wearing?
Did you see or hear anything else in the area at that time?

When was the last time you saw her alive?
What did she say or do then?
Tell me exactly what you did when you saw the body.
Did you touch the body?
What position was the body in?
Do you feel that the girl had any reason to jump?
Had she said anything unusual in the last two weeks?

All those questions and they never asked me if she had any enemies who'd like to push her off a building. I remember that they never asked me that. Maybe they asked her close friends, but not me.

I wrote out my fullest answers to the questions. Yes, I found the body. Almost everything else got a flat no—except my description of her lying there—she wore her green sweater with her initials sewn into it under the neck, a plaid skirt, white blouse and black shoes. The same thing she'd had on in class that day. When I saw her on the concrete I just stared and then ran off to tell Mrs. Howard. Sure, I know Sue Anne—but not too well, and I went home that way because it was a shorter walk than out the front way and Tommy couldn't give me a lift that day because he'd gone home right after his last class and I had to stay for tutorial. The last time I saw her alive was in English class and she didn't say or do anything out of the ordinary there. I remember she giggled and talked some with the other babes—pretty normal if you ask me.

I had told each of the detectives what I saw and heard during it all. Other than seeing King next to his car past the fence behind Mac's shop, I couldn't think of anything else. Especially after I turned the corner—then I just kept looking at what was left of Sue Anne.

In the history class we just finished, everything seemed childish to me. The sophomores passed notes and Jenkins still talked about the Mormons like it actually mattered. The

English class was even worse. I remembered Billy Stephens telling me once that if I thought something was stupid or boring, then tell the teacher that. Like all you had to do was be honest and everything would be great. I told him he was wrong and he just chuckled and said that at least it would make me feel better. But if being honest makes you wind up in the office facing Patton, or if you get beat up, or killed—then it's you who's stupid, not them.

I looked over the questions again and I just couldn't think of anything else. Maybe I'd seen something else and just forgotten. I rubbed my still-bloodshot eyes and thought for a second. I could ask some of her best friends, but they'd just get suspicious and they might not tell me anything anyway. And if they asked me questions back, I really couldn't tell them why I wanted to know without lying to them. I let out a big yawn and a couple people looked at me funny.

What's the point? There was nobody close around when I first saw her on the sidewalk—and I didn't hear her hit. I only saw her after I turned the corner of the tower. She couldn't have been there very long, though. Somebody else would've seen her pretty quickly. I figure three minutes, five minutes tops that she'd been dead.

I saw it again. Her face—the open eyes and her cheek. What was it about that? I just sat back and tried to clear my head for a while. God, it was stifling in that room—and just like I predicted, no one was saying a word or gave another thought about Sue Anne. The babes in the class who cried a bucket of tears at Mallory's Funeral Home for Sue Anne were yapping away—now the only thing they cared about was the shade of their fingernail polish, or what the guys were saying about them, or how they could get a ride in King's car.

Maybe it was just me—because I was the one who saw her like that, the blood coming out of her mouth and her cheek. It flashed before me again, this time a different, clearer focus on her face. The pointed object that came right through her cheek—there was blood all over it. I hadn't known what it was—suddenly, it came to me. It was a black feather that had poked through, probably on impact. And the other feathers around her head—those were probably stuffed in her mouth before she was thrown over. It also explained why there was no scream during her fall. She wasn't awake, maybe not even alive when she was thrown over.

After classes, Tommy and I stood out next to his car and waited for the exit rush to die down. He figured it the same way I did—and he'd been thinking some on his own. I asked him about the feathers in the mouth and again he said that the black feathers were his disgrace and being put in her mouth meant that he could not speak about it to anyone. Another threat. Tommy had asked Ferrito who set the fire and Ferrito couldn't be serious—he was half-wasted and crazy, as usual. "Who do you think, man?" was all he said, laughing. But I had to know more about the feathers.

"Tell me about the feathers—what do they mean for your people?"

He got real quiet again and looked off—but then he pulled himself back and spoke.

"Once you are a brave, you get your first feather. A bright, white feather, not the black feather of disgrace. The bright feathers add up, one for every winter you live through. You can tell how old a brave is by the number of feathers in his headdress."

I could tell it was hard for him to talk about it—probably tough for him to even imagine telling such things to an outsider to the tribe. So I changed the subject and talked about anybody else around that could help us. There just didn't seem to be anybody to ask who wouldn't expect an explanation in exchange for whatever they might know.

"Listen," he said. "You may be right in a lot of your

thinking—but we've been assuming things "

"Like what?"

"Like she was alive when she was fell from the tower—that was a wrong assumption, like you say. And we've been assuming one other thing that we shouldn't."

"What's that?"

"We've been assuming that the killer worked alone."

Thirteen

It was time for me to go and see Billy Stephens again. Tommy walked around to the driver's side of his car and before I started walking away, I saw him stop. He pulled off another black feather that was sticking up from the windshield wiper. He quickly stuffed it down into his pocket and looked over at me. Neither of us had to say a thing. We turned and watched King's red Corvette pull out with Janine in there and Ferrito piled in, too. The heavy metal music blared out and the mirrored sunglasses scanned us as he cruised by. He gunned it and leaned on that horn when he got out on the road.

"I'll see you in an hour at J.B.'s, okay?"

"Okay, I'll wait there for you until your session is over."
Maybe it wasn't right to let him go anywhere alone now, but I really felt like I needed to see Billy this time.

"You look real tired—your eyes are red."
"Yeah—I'm not getting much sleep."
"How come?"
"I don't know—a lot of stuff's been piling up in my head."
"What kind of stuff?"
"Aw, you know—school—and I'm tired of living alone. I mean—that's not what's been making me lose sleep."
"What do you think it is that's been keeping you up?"
"Anxiety, I guess."
There was a long, awkward silence. He just played with his pipe—filling it, tapping it down with his little metal tool, looking at me. It was his way. He figured I'd say what's on my mind when I felt like it.
"A buddy of mine's in trouble."
"You want to say who it is?"
"Yeah—Tommy Elkins."
"He's your best friend, isn't he?"
"Yeah—" More silence.
"What did he do to get into trouble?"
More silence. I couldn't tell him.
"It's no big deal. I don't want to talk about it."
Hearing that, he got up and opened the window to ventilate the place before lighting up. He talked as he struggled with the window sash.
"It must be a big deal if it's keeping you from sleeping. You brought it up, but for some reason—probably an important one—you want to keep it hidden." He came back and sat down, leaned back, lit up and puffed a few times. He looked out the window behind me. Somehow it never bothered me to smell his pipe smoke. "Hey! It's not even you that's in

trouble, right? So what's the big deal?"

"Well, maybe I'm in trouble too—" but then I decided that was all I was going to say.

"Does this have something to do with Sue Anne's death?"

I looked down at the floor.

"Wick—that's kept a lot of people up at night. They don't show it much, but it's still a real strain on them."

"Who's 'them'?"

"Some teachers and a few students who knew her. I can't tell you the names, of course, but I can tell you that even the detectives haven't figured it out."

"How do you know that?"

"Oh, I just know—we counselors aren't always in the dark."

He started playing with his pipe again, looking me over the way he does. I wondered why he wouldn't give me a straight answer to that one.

"You mean they don't know who killed her?"

"Well, essentially, that's it—they don't know."

"How can they be sure she was killed? Or when she died? I mean, whether it was the fall that killed her or not?"

"What?" He stopped himself and sat back before he said anything else. "Do you think it wasn't the fall that killed her?"

There—I'd said too much. I leaned forward, ready to go, to get out of there. Just shut up, Wick.

"Listen, this is serious business. If you have any more information that could help, you've got to—I mean, you really have a moral responsibility to let the police know. It could help crack the case. Either you or Tommy—"

I wanted to try one more thing.

"What we say here is in strict confidence, right?"

"Yes, of course." He hunched forward, puffing. I could tell he was really expecting something.

"Who do the detectives think did it—the real suspects?"

"I—I don't know."

"Do they think it was just one person doing it all?" I wished I hadn't said "it all."

"I don't know that either, but it may well be that others were involved." I was about to ask him where he got his information, but he cut me off.

"Those are my honest answers. I've told you what I know—I realize it's not much. Now I'll appreciate it if you would answer a couple of my questions. That's fair, isn't it?"

"Yeah, that's fair, but I didn't agree to it." I got up to go— we still had half an hour left.

"Hold on now—that's not the way you want to treat this whole matter, is it? We both know you didn't ask for any of this—so if you can't sleep and you're anxious about things, maybe we can work it out here. At least it's worth a shot, isn't it?"

He was always so logical and persuasive. At the door, I spoke.

"You know what you said a while back about death— knowing it—and me about to go through some kind of invisible door?"

"Yes, I remember."

"Well, you may be right."

I walked over to J.B.'s and I didn't know what to tell Tommy. Billy didn't tell me anything, really—and it might have been the wrong thing to do, asking him those questions. We just sat in the car and drank our milkshakes. My eyes were stinging and I was kind of jumpy. No sense talking about the black feather on the windshield either. More taunting, and I didn't know how much more Tommy could take. Who in the hell was doing that? Maybe it was all just a student prank— somebody with an attitude who found out Tommy was a full-blooded Indian and wanted to run him out of the school.

When I asked if that was possible, he just shook his head and then he started up his car. It must've taken ten or twelve times before it caught. We drove on out of J.B.'s and headed toward my place. But I couldn't get the black feathers out of my mind. Sue Anne dead with feathers in her mouth—the black feathers at the fire and in the bathtub. Now, the black feather on the windshield.

God, I needed sleep. We drove down Winrock and suddenly I saw the familiar, black '86 Chevy in front of the apartments. My heart started going again, pounding wildly—I told Tommy to keep on driving. It was him—my dad. I felt dizzy and my chest was so tight that I could hardly breathe.

"What is it? What's wrong!" he shouted, slowing down the car.

"It's my dad—in the apartment. I don't want to see him."

Tommy got to the end of the street and turned right onto Woodway and right again, headed back toward Kirby.

"It's cool—we can go someplace else."

As we drove back out onto Kirby headed nowhere, he started talking, almost to himself. I was better now—I'd gotten away.

"Listen, man—everybody's got something to be scared of. For me, it's somebody with black feathers. For you, it's your old man. My great grandfather, Great-Bow-in-the-Moon, once said that as a boy you have a father, and you do not become a man until you are brave in his presence."

We drove on. I knew that by this time two days from now he would find out if he was brave. Would I ever find out if I was brave?

We headed west on Route 59. The sun was setting, a glowing orange disk streaked with purple and gray, sinking, draining the color out of the sky. Out of nowhere, some drops of water sprinkled the windshield. A few cars heading toward us in the oncoming lanes had their headlights on and the incline in front of us was an arcade of blinking red lights as the cars broke rhythmically, creeping forward in the traffic. The sight transfixed my burning eyes until I slumped over against the window.

Fourteen

One of the turns made me wake up. We were about ten miles west of the school and I suddenly remembered that Shelley told me I could visit her sometime. Now was a good time for me—she'd just have to put up with Tommy too. He wheeled the car off San Felipe and into the Memorial area. Nice neighborhood. Her parents were in London, she'd said. When we pulled up and knocked on the door she took long enough, but she answered. She looked like she was ready for bed.

"Wick! And Tommy—what're you guys doing here?" She looked us up and down and then I realized that we didn't look so great, especially since it had started drizzling on us. Then she had to add, "What's wrong with you?"

"Listen, Shelley—we need a place to stay the night. Don't ask why—if you can't help us out, just say so."

She looked a little startled, but I didn't care.

"Uh, well—sure, you can stay. Just as long as my parents never find out."

"Tommy too."

"Sure, Tommy too."

She didn't look too wild about it, but she let us in as I watched a big, older black woman getting into a car at the other side of the driveway. It was a neatly paved path that went all the way over to the tree line and back out to the road.

"Oh, that's just Eva Mae—she's our cook and cleaning lady."

She took us into the front room and I laid down on the couch. She brought us out some iced tea and Tommy drank his as he sat in a big leather chair with his duffel bag at his feet. I took a sip of mine but I felt so sleepy that I couldn't keep my eyes open. I heard her giggle and Tommy went off to another room. She sat down next to me on the couch and placed a little pillow under my head. I felt her fingers in my hair and I shivered and looked at her face—she looked good, but I couldn't keep my eyes open. It felt like there was sand under my closed eyelids. I saw my father's car still sitting in front of the apartment and I heard some weird, faraway music in my head—the ice cream truck. But I knew it would never come to this neighborhood. I floated in blackness.

I woke up not knowing what time it was or where I was. A blanket was covering me and I felt stiff. For a few moments I just laid there and then I knew—Shelley's house. I heard faint sounds of Tommy and her talking in the next room and I went on in.

"Oh, Wick—Tommy's been telling me about the Sue Anne thing. Gosh! I had no idea it was such a mystery. We've been trying to figure it out."

"We just talked about Sue Anne and nothing else." Tommy said it looking hard at me and I knew what he meant.

"I didn't know her much and nobody asked me about it," she said with real interest, "but I remember she said she was getting a ride home with King that day. She'd have to meet him to do that."

"Did she ever get into his car?" God, my throat was scratchy.

"I doubt it—but I don't really know." She looked at Tommy who just looked back at her.

"Why'd she go to the top of the tower?" I asked.

"I don't know, but it sounds like she didn't go up there to jump off and kill herself. At least not because King changed his mind about giving her a ride home."

"How do you know he did that—changed his mind?" Tommy asked.

"Look, I'm not sure or anything." She looked to me now. "But it's the only thing that makes sense. He met her at the tower and told her to flake off. Either that or he tried to do something to her right there. You know..."

"Yeah, I know. Then what?" My voice still sounded weird to me.

"Well, maybe she said no, or screamed or something and ran up the stairs—I don't know."

Tommy was thinking and he started to rub his eyes as he held his glasses in his hand. "Wick, you said you saw King over across the fence behind Mac's shop with Smeg and Ferrito—"

"Yeah," I said. "I heard they'd been there a while, too. I saw him over there near his car as I came down the sidewalk."

"Cripes! Maybe there's an unknown murderer stalking the school!" She was thrilled with her own exaggeration and didn't really hear me. Then she yawned, putting a hand to her mouth. Nice fingernails.

"He couldn't have done it then—at least not alone," I said.

I closed my eyes and pictured the walk to the back of the school. How did I know so quickly that King's car was over at the shop? Because I could see all the way down the sidewalk from out there. I could see his red Corvette and him standing along side of it, almost as soon as I walked out from Administration Hall. And if I could see him, he could see me.

"You guys want some hot chocolate?" she asked.

We both said yes. Tommy had gotten quiet and when she walked into the kitchen he whispered.

"What is it? What are you thinking?"

"I'm not sure. I—" Then I remembered something else. It seemed silly earlier, but I heard the same old tune playing lightly—the ice cream truck—far out on Windemere Street down from the school. I knew it by heart. That's why I knew there was the honking of a horn from back behind the school—it sounded louder than the faint music. Three honks of the horn as I walked toward the body. Yes, it was clear to me now. I looked off toward the kitchen; she couldn't hear us.

"King was a lookout—whoever threw her off the tower was waiting for the coast to be clear, to be sure that no one was around to see the body fall. Then I walked along, rounded the corner and saw it first."

Tommy nodded. "Yes—I think you're right. If she'd died from the impact with the concrete there'd be more blood than you saw—a lot more if she'd been there awhile." We listened to Shelley clang around in the kitchen. "You heard the horn honk three times as a signal—and you took maybe thirty or forty seconds to get back there—"

"Well, maybe a minute."

"—so, they knew you were coming. It was staged for you, Wick. She was either unconscious or already dead before she was dropped—maybe hit over the head inside the tower. One of those big steel reinforcement bars would do it. She'd be hurt bad if she got hit hard with one of those."

"Yeah—then she could be dragged upstairs and had feathers stuffed in her mouth. There wouldn't be much noise when she hit the concrete and King was just waiting over there behind Mac's shop. King's horn is real distinctive, and at the signal of honking his horn three times, the body was dropped, just waiting there to greet me when I turned the corner. I guess that makes me a big part of King's alibi."

"Yes—and maybe somebody else's alibi, too." He rubbed his eyes again and stretched his arms out in front of him. "So King's probably not the one who hit her."

"Maybe not, but he's sure strong enough to."

"Sure he is, but he wouldn't need to. The violence was done by the one who—" He stiffened for a second and listened for sounds from the kitchen. He didn't need to finish his sentence—I knew what he was going to say.

But who was it that was after Tommy? One of the students? Faculty? A stranger? A blow to the back of the head—it wouldn't take a lot of strength to knock somebody out with one of those thick steel bars, or even to crush a skull.

We heard her walking toward us slowly with the serving tray which held three cups of steaming hot chocolate.

"I hope you guys like marshmallows."

"Sure, that's great," I said. A light rain was falling outside and I looked at the huge grandfather clock in the corner and saw it was already after 1 A.M. No wonder she was yawning. I hoped Tommy had gotten a little sleep, too.

"So, is there any way King did it?" Her eyes were open wide as she sipped her chocolate carefully, but I noticed she looked at my damp clothes and she probably figured I was a first-class slob.

"No—I don't think he could have done it."

"Oh—who did it then?"

"We think it was you, Shelley."

She looked at me, stunned for a second, and then she laughed.

"Right! How'd you figure it out? I wanted to ride with King so bad that I scratched her eyes out, dragged her up to the top of the tower, dropped her down on her head. I confess! Lock me up!" She set down her hot chocolate and held out her hands to be handcuffed.

We all laughed. It helped. I was still real tired and Tommy looked beat. Shelley yawned again.

"Hey! Tomorrow's a school day, remember? And it's after one in the morning. You two guys can sleep in the guest bedroom—we've got twin beds in there. There's an alarm clock in there, too."

Tommy got up, took his duffel bag with him and walked toward the room. When he was gone, she smiled at me. She looked real cute in her flannel nightie.

"Thanks for letting us stay." I remembered her fingers in my hair on the couch and how tired I'd been. "I hope I'm not—we're not bothering you."

"Oh no—I'll be fine. Oh, by the way, Wick…"

"Yeah?"

"You snore a lot."

"Oh…"

She giggled and bounced off to her bedroom. So I snore a lot. Thanks for the tip. I wondered if she was just teasing about wanting to ride with King. I put it out of my mind and went on into the bedroom with Tommy. He and I had a few more things to talk about before we went to sleep. Tomorrow was his last day as a seventeen-year-old.

We didn't say much. We talked a little about a time schedule for the trip, but he was sleepy and I was exhausted, even though everything inside me was racing. Tommy had pulled the curtains closed and now he was asleep. The room had a perfumed kind of smell. The rain had been falling harder and harder, and finally, I drifted into a light sleep.

Later—I don't know how much later—my eyes popped open at the crash of a thunderbolt as the room darkened after a lightning flash. Did I see...? The rain pounded the house and again—a flash of lightning brightened the room through open curtains. I saw him now—standing there in just his jeans in front of the window. His arms were spread-eagled, facing the tremendous storm. It was as if he were drawing strength from the force of the wind, the rain and the fiery sky.

Part Three

 Fifteen

He closed the curtains and laid back down. It was incredible, but in just a few moments he was sound asleep. There was no telling what the next day would hold for him, but he just dropped back off—out like a light.

I just laid there. I could hardly tell if my eyes were open or closed. It was like I could see right through my eyelids. The torrent of rain still lashed at the roof and sides of the house. I felt it as I listened. A soft little breeze hit my face and chest from the air conditioning vent on the far wall.

A dream came upon me. I was turning and dropping—trying to catch onto something as I fell. People were watching me and pointing at me and I was naked. This was a curiosity to them. It went on and on and I slowed down nearly to a stop. Blackness came out of my mouth like ropes of ink. It kept coming and I couldn't stop it. A doctor in a white lab coat kept looking at me. Very serious—could go on for many years. May take a life. It kept on and, after a while, I was being held by the arms and I was shaking.

I awoke with a start. Tommy was shaking me.

"Time to get up, man—we've got to go."

I sat up and rubbed my eyes. So soon? It was just barely light out. We started to get our stuff ready to leave and when Tommy opened the bedroom door I was surprised to hear Shelley out in the kitchen. She must really be an early bird. Tommy went out to the car to check the gas and take his duffel bag out there. I looked out the window and watched him start it up—or at least try. I could tell that it was the same old problem—it just wouldn't catch. Again and again. Stop. Again and again and again. He must've tried the thing over fifty times and he still kept trying it as I went out and stood at the open front door watching him.

"Now what?" I muttered to myself. Tommy just looked over at me and then kept trying. Shelley came up behind me. She looked like she was still a little sleepy herself, standing there in shorts, a shirt and sneakers.

"Nick, if you want to ride with me to school, you can. My brother took the Camaro back to college with him, so I'm taking my mom's car today. It'll get us there a lot better than that old rattle trap."

Tommy was just sitting there in the car, head down.

"Listen, Shelley…"

"Call me Missy—everybody else at the school does."

"Okay, Missy—" Tommy was trying the key again, use-lessly. "We're not going to school today. We've got to take a trip. It's real important."

She was trying to get a grip on the whole thing, but I

couldn't tell her all of it.

"Does this have something to do with Sue Anne?"

"Yeah—it does. But I can't tell you all about it. At least not now. Maybe later. Please, you've got to trust me."

Our eyes locked for a moment and then she shrugged.

"Okay—just take care of the car. I'll get Janine to give me a ride to school."

"That's great—you're really helping us."

She went and got me the keys and I walked over to Tommy to tell him. He'd had that stoic kind of look on his face but now he sighed in relief.

We borrowed two blankets and threw them in the back seat along with his duffel bag and other things. It was a new black Cadillac—the gas tank was full and it started up the first time, purring quietly. It was big, plush and roomy. He turned it off and we went back inside and into the kitchen where Shelley was putting some bread into the toaster. She'd pulled out some cereal, bowls and milk for us for breakfast. Some butter and jam were on the table too.

"You didn't have to do all this," I said.

"Well, you guys have got to eat something." She yawned, covering her mouth. "I've got to get some more sleep or I'll stagger around all day. I'll see you guys when you get back."

Tommy looked at me, wondering what I'd said to her, but we both said goodbye and she went on back to sleep. As we sat down, I noticed a clear plastic bag on one of the chairs. She'd packed us some sandwiches and put four Cokes in it. While we were transferring our stuff into her mom's car, she'd packed it and put in a little note she'd written that I could read through the plastic. "Good luck to Wick and Tommy."

When we'd eaten a little, we put the dishes in the sink and walked out. But then I decided to at least see if she was awake. Tommy went on out with the plastic bag and the keys and I went on back to her room. She had placed a little "Do Not

Disturb" sign on her door—like you see in hotels. I got the message. I walked on out of the house. Tommy had the car started and was ready to go. Soon, we were driving up the on ramp of Highway 59.

"This rides real nice," I said, stretching out.

"It should—it's as big as a boat."

"She's a pretty good gal—" I said it aloud, wanting to hear Tommy's reaction. He just nodded, but then he spoke.

"Yes, she is. She didn't have to let us use this car. She knows something is up, too. She's pretty smart. Maybe you better hang onto her."

"Yeah—" It was his way of teasing me, but it felt good to hear him say it. She was great about everything, and the sandwiches and Cokes would taste good along the way.

"What do you think she's doing at Leary if she lives way out in Memorial and she's smart?"

"She was flunking a few subjects at Lamar and her parents panicked."

"Is that all?"

"Yeah, that's all. You get all types at Leary—you know."

The road was almost dry by now but I could see that the gullies on the side roads were still full. Highway 59 headed south and west and nothing but nine hours of driving lay in front of us. And that was just the beginning of the Indian land. Only Tommy knew exactly where to go once we got there. We'd take turns driving.

I turned on the radio and we listened to some crazy DJ a little while. It was a crummy looking morning. After about a half an hour, Tommy started talking a little about it. What the reservation was like, what he would do when he got there, but he was vague—or I was just tired, I don't know. It sounded like it all depended on what he ran into when he got there— he really didn't know what to expect. Honor was all that seemed to matter. He made it sound like he would be facing some kind of fight. I couldn't help, he said—like it was some kind of personal quest for him. Both of us were still a little sleepy and if we were going to be driving, some caffeine might help.

"You want some coffee or a donut or something?"

"Sure, that'd be good—might keep me awake at the wheel."

Good. I felt a little sick to my stomach, being awakened in the middle of sleep. We were out of the city limits now and it was another three miles or so to the next exit. Tommy kept the car rolling smoothly down the road—just a couple of fingers on the wheel was all it took with that sensitive power steering. The way he focused straight ahead, he seemed like he was in some kind of trance.

I started to doze a little, another half-sleep. And then it came—slowly, almost creeping on me. I felt fear—like something touching the right side of my face. Then suddenly—it clutched my hair. I screamed and Tommy ran off the road, brakes screeching as we hurtled off the shoulder and into the high grass.

Sixteen

The jolt threw Shelley right over the seat and onto the floor in front of me.

"God! What're you—" but my words stopped as her feet hit me right in the face. She started to pull herself up so she was facing me.

"Oh—hi! I just wanted to surprise you. Tommy, you didn't have to stop that fast!"

But he was busy looking behind us at the empty—and cop-less, thank God—highway. He pulled the car back onto the highway and got up to speed. But I could see him shaking his head at the whole thing. She scrambled up to sit between us.

"Owww—I bumped my head." She looked at me for sympathy and didn't get any.

"Shelley—" I looked at her and past her and saw Tommy still shaking his head no. The exit was coming up and we eased off and pulled in to a twenty-four-hour gas and quick-eats place. We all got out and I went over to Tommy as he walked toward the restaurant. She followed right next to me.

"Look Shelley, we need to talk alone. You shouldn't have done this." She looked at me kind of guilty and hopeful at the same time. I turned and went in the door to talk to Tommy.

He just stood there shaking his head. "No way, man. No way. We've got to get her back, pronto. It's the only way."

"Yeah, you're right. I'll tell her." But then she walked in the door and stood there a few feet from us, a defiant look on her face. Tommy turned his back to her and faced me. "Look—I don't care what she says, it's just too dangerous. I don't know what's going to happen out there. She could be hurt—or worse. You don't want to live with that, man."

She just walked up and tapped me on the shoulder. "Look, I'm not going to be a pest or anything, but where the car goes, I go. It's Mummy's car and it's not going anywhere without me."

He just rolled his eyes and looked quickly at me before he turned away and walked over to the nearest bar stool at the counter.

"Look, Shelley—I mean, Missy—you said we could use the car and you never said anything about coming along. And I know it's a lot to ask, but we can't let you come with us. We just can't—please trust me. There may be real trouble and we don't want you to get hurt." But I could tell that this just excited her more. We were forty-five minutes outside of the city and this was Tommy's only way to get out to the reservation today. She knew all that.

"If it's so important, then he needs the car, and Mummy'll

kill me if I let anything happen to her Cadillac. Maybe it's already scratched up from running off the road!"

"Yeah—thanks to you hiding in the back seat and scaring the crud out of me." She just folded her arms in front of her.

"Look—the car goes where I go and that's it. You can take me back home, but you'll never get his old junker fixed in time to get out to the reservation before that stupid deadline I heard you guys talking about."

So—now I knew she'd listened at the door to at least part of our conversation in the bedroom last night.

"You might as well take me—I'll bring you good luck!" She winked at me.

I went over to Tommy and he'd already figured it out. It was weird with him. I knew how much he hated that she was coming along. If ever there was strictly a man's business, this was it. I felt that way too. But there was nothing we could do now and he accepted it when I told him. Just one hurdle after another. It was as if all of nature were working against him, making the quest more difficult than anyone could have imagined.

In twenty minutes we were back on the road, the three of us sipping our hot coffee through plastic lids we'd torn holes in after we'd eaten our jelly donuts. We'd have been out of there in fifteen minutes, but Shelley had to go into the john to put on her makeup. We were losing the radio stations from the city but she found a station that played pretty good music, along with news and farm and market reports. We were cruising right through some farmer's pasture—cattle were grazing on both sides of us. The sun was up and bright now.

"So you think I'm a pretty good gal, huh Wick?" She jabbed me with an elbow, trying to embarrass me.

"It's not enough you're sneaky, you've got to eavesdrop, too, huh?"

"Yep, that's me!" She grinned and winked at me. "Nosy

and sneaky…" She said it like it was a big joke. Tommy wasn't talking, even when she spoke to him.

"…and you think he should hang onto me, right, Tommy?"

I swear, he just looked at her—like he was suddenly real old, the way you'd look if you were listening to a child. He was just patient and quiet.

"Well…" she said, turning back to me. "At least you didn't start talking about my physical attributes." She said it slowly, sticking her legs out together in front of me and smoothing down her shorts. "Eeks! I didn't even have time to shave my legs before I went bounding off into the wilderness." She looked at me for approval. I smiled. I mean, she's got real good legs.

It went on like that for a while, but it seemed like the only thing that mattered was the miles we were eating up. Tommy kept it right at sixty miles an hour most of the time, but on the long, vacant straightaways he got up over seventy. We didn't see any cops and not too many cars. After a couple of hours her head rested against my shoulder, eyes closed.

Farm and weather reports on the radio, grassy farmland and gently rolling hills after Brookshire. Tommy and I did our own thinking. I wondered what it would be like to live out here. Later, I remembered what Tommy had asked me about Shelley—about why she was at Leary. Like he really didn't believe that her low grades were the problem. He had a way of knowing about things like that. Her head popped up after a while and she squirmed and stretched as silently as she had laid her soft brown hair against my shoulder.

"You still sleepy?" I asked her.

"Uh-huh." She looked around with interest, but seeing nothing, she sat back.

"Missy, you were telling me that you came to Leary because your grades were low."

"Yep. Flunking three subjects. Daddy and Mummy figurcd it'd be a lot easier at Leary."

"Well, I guess you're right there." But she looked at me in a funny kind of way and she knew that I knew there were ways to beat that. "Daddy and Mummy" could afford an expensive private tutor to get her through that.

"There's something else, isn't there?" I turned to face her as I asked.

"What do you mean?"

"You know what I mean. A lot of us at Leary have some personal stuff that doesn't smell so great. You wanted to come on this trip and tricked us both to do it. So tell us—what's your rap?"

She just sat there real offended and got red in the face. She was embarrassed and angry, too.

"You don't believe me, do you?"

"No, I don't."

She looked to Tommy, but he didn't take his eyes off the road. Then she got real quiet, but she knew it wouldn't work. We were looking at another five hours together in the car, but if she could just walk away right then, she'd do it. She turned to me after a few minutes; her face was defiant but her lower lip was trembling.

"Okay—I got busted—three times. Shoplifting. Swim-suits, bracelets, stuff like that. First time, a warning. Second time, it's on your record. Third time you get a choice—women's detention center or probation and rehab at a low-class hole like Leary." She spat out the last few words. "Satisfied?" Hate covered her face now.

Wonderful. I wanted to know and now I knew. We were crazy, each of us. Crazy as we sat there and crazy for driving off to who-knows-where to get into who-knows-what kind of trouble. It was like some kind of weird movie or something. You get thrown in with people that nobody'd ever dream up and if they did, you wouldn't want to sit next to them in a car.

Great. Just great. A runner, a thief, and Tonto—hellbent for the end of the road.

Seventeen

We drove on. I'd asked him three times if he wanted me to drive some and he just said no. The driving seemed to help his concentration. Somewhere past Titusville we ate our sandwiches and drank our Cokes. A change seemed to come over the land. It was barren now. The green seemed faded and sparse out on the prairie and dark clouds streaked the horizon. It was late afternoon and the car was dusty and gritty—when the wind kicked up you could hear the grit against the windows. It hadn't rained here yesterday.

"God! How far is it?" she asked.

"An hour or so more," Tommy said.

We filled up with gas back at Terralingus three hours ago

and Tommy and I got out and talked. Maybe I should say we just stood next to each other. Now we pulled up to a little nothing of a place called Two Bit and got out again and stretched. Shelley had just crawled onto the back seat and stayed there, trying to sleep. For a while, I felt like opening the door and telling her that she snored even though she didn't. The sun looked grotesque hanging there above the road. Dust in the air made it look like some colored paper pasted on a gray wall. Two pickup trucks were parked there outside the little general store and saloon. Tommy quietly went into his duffel bag in the back seat and pulled some things out while I went to the john.

Inside, there was a dark-skinned man wearing a gimme cap and sitting on a stool. He was so still sitting there with his bottle of beer that he could've been a statue. The white-haired man behind the counter looked me over when I asked him where the john was. He waited a long time and I watched his unshaven face and his lips working over his toothless gums. He jerked a thumb behind him off to the side. I said I'd be just a minute and he practically snarled back.

"The world ain't gonna wait for ya, kid."

Jeez—the old guy knew me for twenty seconds and he hated me already. What's wrong with people?

When I got back out from the filthiest men's room I'd ever seen, Tommy was walking back from the mailbox outside the front of the store.

"Ready?" he asked.

"Sure—how 'bout you?"

He nodded and looked down the road. "Try to keep her in the car if you can."

"Right."

He looked behind us back up the road like he'd been doing. The little crossroad we'd gotten off onto was only about ten miles off Highway 59, but it might as well have been three hundred miles off it. We traveled the two-lane road of cracked pavement, bumping along, the air-conditioner whirring softly inside and the air outside purple and thick in the distance.

Up ahead we could see the sign telling us the land was a reservation site. As we were coming up to it, Tommy eased off the road and followed a dirt path that led far away from the established part of the reservation. There was a wire fence that had been knocked down and he followed the path over it. It got real bumpy and Shelley woke up.

"God! Why can't you stay on the road?"

"We're on the reservation now," I said.

"Well, where is everybody?"

I've never seen a place so deserted. It wasn't just natural prairie land. There was trash blowing around where people had been and broken bottles and blackened spots of dead campfires. Tommy carefully guided the car around a few knolls and off in the distance there were some little shacks. Off in the opposite direction I could see a small grove of pine trees next to several low mounds.

Tommy stopped the car and took out his duffel bag. I got out of the car and watched as he tore off his shirt with a savage ripping of his hands. He reached back into the bag and took one of the black feathers around which he had tied a string of horsehide. He wrapped it around his head, the feather sticking up in back. He strapped his sheathed knife up to his belt at the right hip.

I stepped back. He dipped each of three fingers individually in a little tin of some kind of soot and streaked his cheeks with sharp, slashing motions. And then he made some kind of sound—a sound I've never heard before, and he raised his arms slowly in front of him as he faced the setting sun. He didn't look like Tommy anymore—whatever he was now, he was different. We got in and he drove over to the pine tree grove. Behind it were three pickup trucks in the clearing. Men got out of each of the trucks as we pulled up. Something looked familiar, somehow. They were dark-skinned, stripped to the waist, too. Two of them wore beads. I watched them, four in all, walk up to our car as we stopped.

Tommy got out of the car and walked up to them, facing the group. I started to get out, too.

"Wait, Wick—don't! I'm scared. What do they want with Tommy?"

"I don't know. Stay in the car."

"Wait—"

I got out, slammed the door and stood at the front of the car. Then Tommy let out a shout—high pitched, rapid. His own language. It actually frightened me to hear him do it. The black-haired men with dark, heavy faces just looked at him and then me. They understood the weird language. One of the men motioned to two others and they walked to the car, opened the doors and jerked out his duffel bag. They pulled out the contents, examined each article, and threw it all on the ground.

Tommy never turned, even when Shelley gave out a yelp and ran out of the car and up to me. My mind raced. Had Tommy left the keys in the ignition?

After they'd emptied the bag and searched everything else in the car, they went back to the others. They hadn't found the papers. What had Tommy done with them? What would they do now?

Tommy screamed out his native words again and he pointed to one of the trucks. I looked over and there was one other man in the truck I hadn't noticed. Everything stopped until finally, the man got out. He was short and stocky with dark hands and arms, and he wore a faded shirt. He had on a drooping straw hat that almost covered and totally shaded his face. He came slowly over to us and when he stepped forward, there was something about his walk. Tommy burst out again with his words and he ripped the feather and strap off his head and threw it at the man's feet. I could tell now that he was challenging the man to show who he was—if he was honorable. And I knew the man would do it, even with me and Shelley there. It was their way.

Tommy shouted out the same words again and made the gestures to his face—like he did with the soot. Then they stood in silence. Like they were the only two people in the world. The man in the hat was the killer—and from that moment onward I would always wonder if, as the man's hand reached up to take off the hat, if we could have just dashed back into our car and driven out of there. Made a run for it.

The wind threw the gritty air at us as the thick hands pulled the hat down from the head of Mendoza—the Keowahk Indian.

Shelley gasped. "It's the janitor guy at the school."

Mendoza heard her and turned to us. Then he spoke to Tommy in English.

"You have brought the white man here to disgrace us, Great-Bear-in-the-Forest. You will never survive the trial of the earth. All of you die." He shouted commands in his native tongue and the men grabbed Tommy.

Eighteen

It happened so fast. I just looked in horror as they dragged him over to the old green truck, taking his knife from him before he could use it. They forced him to the ground and pulled ropes from the truck, tying his hands together behind him and his feet together—then they tied his hands to his feet and secured the rope around the back bumper of the truck. I went weak all over and my heart raced. I couldn't breathe. Then I heard him scream—

"Wick! Get away! Both of you—GO!"

The truck engine roared with Mendoza at the wheel and it took off, jerking Tommy after it—crashing him against the hard, sun-baked ground. When I heard my name I snapped to—I ran to the car and jumped inside. The keys were there! I turned the ignition and started it as one of the men grabbed at the door. It was my chance to get away. I shot forward, knocking him away, and I pulled the door closed and locked it. I drove straight at the other men and they scattered, with one falling off to the side, the tires bumping over his legs.

One of the men had grabbed Shelley, and I turned toward them, not knowing what to do—but then she kicked him in the shin and broke away, running toward me.

"Get in and lock the doors—" She catapulted into the seat against me and jumped to lock the door.

"Oh my God—get us out of here, Wick. Did you see—" She was gasping for breath. "Just go home now—"

I turned the wheel toward the green truck and gunned it. The Indians were running to their trucks.

"Wh-what're you doing? The road's that way! Turn around!"

Off in the distance, I saw the helpless, bound form of Tommy spinning and crashing into the dirt and rocks behind Mendoza's truck. Then the Indians pulled out shotguns. I threw her forward with my arm.

"Get down—on the floor—they've got—"

I felt the explosion as the back window burst toward us. Glass flew into me and ricocheted off the dashboard. I heard her moan from the carpet.

"Oh—Mummy's car—ohh…"

"Stay down!" I saw a flash of red behind me near the trees. What was it? The two other trucks started up and came at us.

"Oh—please, no—just go home. Please…"

I looked over my shoulder and saw it now. The red Corvette. It was King coming slowly around the pines. But I had to stop that green truck that pulled Tommy. I gunned it and went at the truck, circling from the side—closer, closer. He turned when he saw me and started to back up, but he was too slow. I careened into him—a tremendous crash broadside, knocking the truck onto two wheels and then over onto its side. Glass and steam flew up in front of me and the jolt threw me against the wheel, almost knocking me out. The windshield flew into a thousand pieces around us as Shelley shook in terror on the floor.

My car was still running, so I backed away—I saw the two other trucks coming toward me. I felt the blood running down my face from the broken glass and a sharp pain split my chest. Quickly, I steered away from the wrecked truck. My hood was crumpled in front of me and I expected another collision, but one of the trucks peeled off and drove past me toward the village—the other swerved around behind the overturned truck. The Indian, shotgun still in hand, got out and used the butt of the rifle to knock out the remaining windshield glass and pull out Mendoza, bloody and cursing. They got into the running truck and drove off, following the other truck. I stopped the car. My chest was agony and the taste of blood was in my mouth as I leaned back against the seat. Shelley got out of the car and started staggering away. I called to her. But then I swallowed hard because I heard that turbo-charged V-8 engine rev up—faster—faster. King tore out, heading straight toward us.

"Shelley—c'mon, get back in—Shelley!"

But she didn't hear me. She held her head in her hands, crying.

"SHELLEY!"

He was really moving now—head on. I pressed down on the accelerator—it was my only chance. But with my speed I couldn't...

He roared up, turning not at me, but at her—and I swerved with a quick jerk as the engine screamed at the final effort to catch him—must hit him—

The crash was nearly head on, just ten yards in front of

her. It knocked his car up off the ground and tore its fiberglass body to pieces, throwing me against the wheel again. The tires on the 'Vette spun crazily before it landed back flat on the ground. I saw King crawl out holding his head and putting his sunglasses back on quickly. He looked okay.

Shelley keeled over in the dirt in front of us. She was vomiting. He stood up—panting, glaring at me as I got out of the car. The last rays of sun glinted on his mirrored glasses as he sucked in his breath and came at me.

I don't know what happened to me then. I didn't think I could even move, but I threw myself forward and rammed into his chest, knocking us both into the dirt.

"Hey, man—I wasn't—" he grunted, "—trying to hit your girl. Hey!"

I hit him in the face and his glasses flew off. He yelled at me to stop, flailing his arms. Suddenly, he grabbed my ear and started to rip—No! The pain—but then, before he could finish, I pounded him hard in the chest. He tried to slither away but I grabbed his leather jacket and held him down. I saw him now—he was cross-eyed and weak.

"Tell me all of it, you piece of scum—NOW!"

"I didn't kill Sue Anne—Mendoza did—I was just the lookout. He told me to follow you here and he'd give me three thousand bucks for helping out. I swear, man—" He fumbled to find his glasses but I grabbed them and broke them in my hands. I threw them in his dirty face.

I got up and he crawled away toward the pine trees, apologizing and covering his face as the wind kicked up the grit again. I could think clearly now. The Cadillac was gone. If anything would run it would be King's Corvette. I took the keys out of his ignition and went over to Shelley. She was practically in shock now—hurt and sick.

Together, we walked over to Tommy. He was shoved up against the tailgate—his hands and feet were still tied. He was a quiet, bloody hulk now. His battered face was cocked against a bare shoulder. His eyes were closed, not seeing the growing darkness. I told Shelley to go back and get a blanket to cover him and then I untied the ropes from the truck and from his broken body. When she got back I knelt and started to weep as I covered him. He was a man of honor—a true brave. He would live with his fathers.

Nineteen

A few days later, the truth came out for everybody. The aftermath would be a life sentence for Mendoza—a clever, angry Keowahk Indian who was fluent in three languages—English, Spanish and the ancient tongue of the Keowahk tribe. Yet he could never make it in the white man's world. He sold himself out to another Indian tribe, offering to get them the Keowahk land "by any means possible." He'd tracked down Tommy "Great-Bear-in-the-Forest" Elkins and lived out the role of the Leary school janitor for three years. He'd flooded Tommy's trailer and even let himself get burned by the fire he'd set in his janitor's room at Leary. Nobody had suspected him.

On that fateful night, Shelley did get to ride in King's car—only it was with me over to the little Keowahk village, and there was almost no body left on the Corvette. We had watched King as he cowered off in the pine trees. It came out later that he'd told Sue Anne he'd take her with him over to the mall if she'd meet him after school in the tower. Mendoza hit her from behind. King was old enough to serve the expected three to five years in the state pen for being an accessory to murder.

Yesterday, Shelley (she didn't want me to say "Missy" anymore) showed me a few bruises and cuts she had, but nothing serious. She'd brought my school books and a little bouquet of flowers to me here in the hospital. I could tell by the way she talked that she'd had enough trouble for a while. She planned to fly straight now. She also told me that her mother had full insurance on the car and they'd get a new one just like it. And get this—she leaned over and kissed me. It was just like I figured—she's a great kisser.

My wounds would take a little while to heal—some stitches in the head, two bruised and three broken ribs. My ear really hurts, too. It's okay—the pain pills help. I spent a lot of time talking to a newspaper reporter (who'd brought a photographer with him to take pictures of me) and to that young detective from the city police force. And I got more attention from the people at Leary than I ever thought possible—even a note from Dr. Nealon. I've been thinking about the school. I really wondered if they'd ever get those spray-painted letters off the brick wall—I mean, since Mendoza's gone now. Anyway, if those guys at Lamar ever want to know the real answer to "Whatever Happened at Leary High?"—I'm the one to ask.

When that young detective came by yesterday to congratulate me and talk, before he left, I asked about Tommy. He said the council of the tribe had complete jurisdiction there. Tommy had been buried in accordance with their customs—before the sun set the following day at their sacred burial mounds. It sounded like they respected Tommy and that all of his tribal rights were honored.

My dad read the newspaper article and came by to see me. When I talked to him, somehow I didn't feel afraid. In fact, I don't feel like running anymore. We talked a little while and when he asked me if he could do anything for me, I made my request simple—quit drinking. You know what? He was the one who got short of breath and had to leave in a hurry.

When I first got to the hospital the doctors were looking for internal injuries—there weren't any—and my mom came rushing in from out of town. I started to tell her the story but she was so nervous that she did most of the talking. Along with my toiletries, she brought me my mail from the apartment and there was a large yellow envelope in it that just had my name and address on the outside. Inside it were all the legal papers that Tommy had been carrying around in his duffel bag. He had signed them in several places about a week before his birthday and had them all notarized. He'd put them all in the big envelope and mailed them to me. I realized now what he was doing at that mailbox outside the little general store at Two Bit.

The papers were folded around one feather. It looked like it might have been a feather from a dove—beautiful and white. I noticed that there was one blank line left to sign on most of the papers.

Ol' Billy Stephens would be coming to visit me in about half an hour. I would really enjoy telling him the whole story. He's one who really deserved to hear it. I guess he was right. Sometimes we pass through invisible doors in life and we don't know until later that we've passed through them. I had passed through one—and somehow, I knew that things would never be quite the same again. Even as I laid there in the hospital bed answering questions and getting my picture taken, I knew that I was different now—changed, just like Tommy had been changed into a young Indian brave. It was an incredible feeling.

I had to stop, blink my eyes, and think for a little while. I could simply start signing my name and legally, I would be the new chief of an Indian nation.